For Sheelagh with love

FORGIVING THYME

Elisabeth C. Thompson

E C Thompson.

Forgiving Thyme

ISBN: 978-1-908128-75-1

For Emma

One who has journeyed
in a strange land
cannot return unchanged

C.S. Lewis

CHAPTER 1

Rain hung in the air. The sky light as pearl and then heavy as slate as the sun slid behind the clouds like the backdrop in some small-budget drama. The one-handed clock on the tower of St. Laurence-on-the-Hill struck two; the Reverend Jon Driver glanced up at its ghostly face, his tall frame silhouetted against the church in the wintry half-light. Money was on his mind; not the love of it but how to raise a significant amount.

His path to this parish had been a tortuous one. He had fought against his calling until the voices nagging his psyche had reached a tumult. It was only after his ordination that he realised he was finally free of their clamour.

He had laughed out loud when the Bishop suggested St Laurence-on-the-Hill. It was only a stone's throw from his childhood home at the rectory of St. Giles where his father had been in charge for years. To have tried to escape his fate, to have travelled so far only to have ended up where he started, appealed to his sense of the ridiculous. His father had understood his vacillation; he would have appreciated the irony of his preferment.

Daisy Parsloe had revealed the church accounts to him on his first day. He knew exactly what he had taken on at St. Laurence's; soon there would be a second meeting. He had promised to come up with more suggestions to raise funds for the replacement organ but so far no nice little earners had sprung to mind.

His fingers trailed through the streak of blonde hair that had provoked so much comment in his youth. If it had not caused prospective conquests to swoon, it had certainly given him an edge over his peers. Now, like his wild spirit, it had been tamed; camouflaged amongst the premature greying of the rest of his hair which was longer than the norm and without a nod to style or fashion.

He decided not to waste his precious few minutes of spare time re-visiting the aborted mission ... and anyway, he was sure the resourceful Daisy would have her own solutions to that problem. Tucking his hands into the stiff leather of his bomber jacket he headed for Sue's Place and the promise of a pot of Lapsang Suchong.

Daisy Parsloe wheeled her bike out of the shed and lent it against the garden wall while she locked up. It was one of those days, she thought, when you knew it was only going to get colder. She was sorry that Jon Driver had received a chilly welcome to the parish. The climate in church was as glacial as a Polar Bear's pallet with the heating still out of action and she had no intention of lingering there longer than was necessary. What with that and the lack of money in the coffers she reckoned he must be a saint to have agreed to take on the challenge of St. Laurence-on-the-Hill.

It was her turn to organise tea and chat. She did not know in what state she might find the kitchen at the hall; it was let out to various groups during the week, some tidier than others. Once there were clean cups and saucers ready and the urn bubbling away, she could relax and concentrate on fund-raising issues. The expense of the new heating system had been a challenge but the added cost of a replacement organ would try her fiscal skills to the limit and in her role of Treasurer she had to find a way of helping to raise the cash for both.

She balanced astride the saddle and dropped her leather satchel into the basket. It swayed to and fro like a barrel-chested gymnast as she tugged at her gloves and linked fingers cog-like to stretch them into place. After adjusting her hat into an easier position under the helmet, she dipped her chin and started pedalling.

She checked her watch as she approached the church, its over-large face easy to read despite the glowering clouds; the journey had taken precisely five minutes and twenty-three seconds. That was about average if she managed to sail down the bridge over the river like a derny rider at the track. If she had to cut her speed for Sunday drivers or a tractor full of hay it could be nearer seven minutes. She gripped the brakes, slowing down as she coasted in and bumped to a halt against the kerb.

There was a young woman loitering on the pavement by the church. "Can I help?" she called as she dismounted. The woman did not appear to have heard. She scooted round to the back of the hall, slotted the bike into one of the racks and retrieved her satchel from the basket. Peering round the corner she saw the woman move nearer the doors. Her stilted steps reminded Daisy of the walkie-talkie doll her cousin Lynne had been given in the sixties. She kept up her surveillance as she recalled the plaintive 'mamas', the clicking of plastic knees and the hours they had spent playing happy families. Taking a hand each, they would swing the doll between them or clutch the hard fingers to persuade it to goose step up and down the garden in pink-bowed shoes ... happy days.

Back in the present she watched the young woman finger one of the iron rings set in the centre of the heavy oak doors. They were always left unlocked for 'passing trade' as Jon Driver had decreed, despite Owen grumbling about light-fingered villains. Owen grumbled about most things, she thought dismissively. She did not know why he bothered. He must have noticed that no-one paid any heed to his grumbling.

She speculated as to why the young woman was standing on the threshold instead of going inside out of the cold ... even without heating it would be a few degrees warmer in there ... and she wouldn't know the heating was on the blink anyway.

She considered approaching her to explain about the new vicar's 'open door' policy and then marvelled at her ability to stand so still ... still as one of the white-faced artists she had encountered at the Cross in Linchester, bandaged and immobile until they changed position and startled the crowd. She waited, preparing herself for the unexpected. All of a sudden the young woman turned her back on the doors and re-traced her steps. It was then that she noticed the parcel tucked under her arm.

Daisy was about to leave too, but as she wavered the woman returned, walking swiftly now and with more purpose. She heard the handle turn with its familiar iron-clad clunk and then she saw it yield. She watched as the young woman disappeared inside.

She tried to fix a description of her in her mind. Young, slim, shoulder-length hair, parka-style coat, dark tights, ankle boots. She didn't look like one of Owen's imagined villains but you could never be sure these days, she thought, remembering the old lady she had seen apprehended outside the jewellers in the shopping mall, her sparrow legs desperate to make a get-away from the security guard blocking her path. There was a tussle and her draw-string bag coughed up its haul of expensive watches onto the block paviors.

She considered the parcel. She visualised a hack-saw set alongside skeleton keys, a screwdriver and a pair of pliers, all wrapped like a panino in the brown paper camouflaged as an opportunist's packed lunch. She let herself into the hall and decided that when she had finished with the urn she would check the jar of coppers sitting on a window sill in the west aisle ... and then she would see if any of the silver had been disturbed.

Thyme Sykes sat down behind a pillar at the back of the

church and placed the parcel on the seat beside her. She dropped to her knees while the organ mumbled into its stops like an old man muttering into his beard; she knew that time was running out for the cracked pipes and winded console ... no-one could have failed to notice the enormous 'Support our Organ Fund' banner suspended from the rafters over the centre aisle. She lifted her head as it squealed like a skidding car and then fell silent. The organist leaned across the console to remove his score. He switched off the light, slid down from the organ stool and left through the vestry door without noticing her.

When he had gone, she hoisted herself from the cushioned kneeler onto one of the wooden chairs that had replaced the carpeted pine pews some years before, at the same time raising her eyes to the altar and then to the wooden effigy of Christ staring down at her. She continued to gaze up at the outstretched arms; she contemplated the anguished features as she tried to formulate a meaningful supplication. The words crowding her mind would not form sensible sentences.

She was tired. Tired of smiling when she was sad inside, tired of listening to the minutiae of other people's lives and trying to make sense of her own; tired of life in general. If she had a prayer it was to be relieved of her burden, to feel happy in her life, to come to terms with the past. She had hoped to find some sort of peace here, a salve for her wounded psyche but there was nothing. She could not even appreciate the beauty of the stained glass windows or the glorious floral arrangements. She did not take in the magnificence of the rood screen or the fierce glare of the carved eagle on the lectern.

The silence in the church oppressed her. The walls seemed to be moving in on her like the spikes of an iron maiden. Panic rose in her chest and as she struggled to breathe she questioned why she had thought this might have helped when nothing else had. The emptiness inside was a constant reminder of what she had done; nothing could change that. She had been foolish to think it might. She picked up the parcel and fled.

CHAPTER 2

Angela Reedman had switched off. Owen was singing the praises of the new vicar and she had heard more than enough. "I think we made the right choice," he finished with a self-satisfied smile.

She knew he wanted approbation, for her to acknowledge how right he had been in backing the Bishop's selection of Jon Driver but she didn't feel inclined to pander to his ego. "So you approve of him," she said re-aligning the tortoiseshell combs either side of her head.

"Of course I do. He's promised to sort out the new organ and encourage a younger element into the church without alienating the rest of us. I've heard him preach and he can give a good sermon. That's a plus." She gathered bacon and mushrooms from the well-stocked fridge without making comment. Lunch had fallen behind. "David said he was in the running club at school. He was friends with Tom Briggs years back."

"Is he married?"

"Didn't you read the blurb I gave you?"

She remembered the sheaf of papers now filed away with the kindling for their log burner and tried not to look guilty. Since he had retired he liked to keep himself busy. She had no objection to that but he always wanted others to appreciate how busy he was and she found that tiresome; also the fact that, now he was church warden, he carried files around with him at all times, doling out a portion of the contents whenever and wherever he perceived the need. They had become like a badge of office making him feel more important than he deserved to be. "Not all of it," she admitted.

He sighed. "He's not married, but I think that's all to the good. He'll be able to concentrate on church matters ... no conflict of interest. I think you'll like him."

"It's neither here nor there what I think," she said. "I won't have much to do with him, will I?" Her eyes gleamed as she cracked two eggs and tipped them into the frying pan. "But I don't want him to think me unfriendly. We must have him round for a meal. I'll invite Georgia."

"You're not match-making again, Angela. We don't want a repeat of the Mrs. Boyle saga," he said, bulbous eyes delivering a disapproving glare.

"Georgia is hardly Mrs. Boyle; she's only twenty-five and she hasn't had one decent relationship in her life. I know that's what she wants, she told me so the other day when she came round to cut my hair."

"I think our granddaughter is quite capable of choosing her own men."

"Of course she is but she doesn't see past the pectorals and it always ends in tears. She needs someone more ... more ..."

He sucked the last few drops of tea from the ends of his droopy moustache. "You mean someone with more than cotton wool between his ears."

"No," she said reflectively. "More mature, that's what I mean."

With the urn bubbling away issuing its steamy warmth into the church hall it was comfortable enough for the ladies to have removed their coats. They were huddled round the beech table like a covey of grouse, tea and cake in front of them, bags set on the floor close by.

"The money will flood in when everyone hears what we're planning to do," Daisy said. "That man is a phenomenon, a breath of fresh air."

"We were lucky to have found him," Marion Grey said.

"We didn't find him," Rachel Meeks said. "That was down to the Bishop."

"Same difference," Daisy replied.

"I hope you don't think I'm donating anything to the organ fund," she added. "I've put my name down for one of his books and that's it. I barely have enough to manage these days," she said, diamonds glinting in her ears and her treble chin wobbling alarmingly.

"I thought you'd just been on a cruise," Daisy said.

Rachel pulled both sides of her cardigan over her ample bosom where it stayed for two seconds before curling back to the boundaries. "John paid for that."

No-one commented. They all knew that although they had been married for nearly forty years, Rachel and John Meeks led separate and very different lives.

"Well, perhaps *he* would like to contribute," Vi Tracey said, trying to ignore the impatient tapping of Rachel's toe against the table leg as she waited for more tea.

"I doubt it."

"It doesn't have to be money," Daisy said. "I've decided to set up a fund-raising committee. I'm meeting the vicar later to discuss it. Does anyone want to help with that?"

"I will, put my name down," Vi said. "We could have a jumble sale; they always do well round here."

"We'll need several if we want to raise a fair amount," Rachel said, stuffing in the last of the rock buns.

"If the vicar agrees, I'll put a suggestion box at the back of the church. It might take a while but we'll do it. You just have to have faith."

Rachel coughed as a crumb went down the wrong way. "Faith, my eye," she said. "It's cash we'll need and lots of it."

"Rachel, that's a terrible thing to say," Joan Drabble squeaked from behind the tea urn. "If we don't have faith, what do we have?"

"You're both right," Daisy said. "We'll need faith and a considerable amount of money."

Marion Grey had been listening quietly. "Let's have a raffle. I can make one of my cakes. Everyone loves my fruit cakes."

Daisy smiled. "That's more like it. If we set it all up by Easter it could be a Simnel cake."

"I'll speak to Bella. She's good at raffles."

"I'm happy to round up donations from the local shops," Daisy said. "See what she says."

"Perhaps we could persuade Angela to make some of her cards. I know she doesn't come to church, but her cards are very popular," Marion went on. "We could have an Easter Craft Fair and a raffle."

"Here's your tea," Joan said as she scuttled over to Rachel with the replenished cup. "I've got a bottle of red wine you can put in the raffle. My nephew bought it for me at Christmas. It's a good one. He's something in the City."

"Why don't *you* drink it?" Rachel said. "Red wine's good for you. John and I always have a glass with our evening meal ... when he's here."

Joan shrugged her shoulders. "I've never been much of a drinker and Fred prefers beer."

"It's very generous of you," Daisy said. "Are there any other offers?"

"I'll go on the committee if Owen isn't on it," Marion said. "He'll just take over."

"I know what you mean but we can't stop him if he's really keen."

"Making him church warden was a mistake," Rachel said. "It's completely gone to his head. I don't think he knows the meaning of consensus."

"He is a silly man but his heart's in the right place," Vi said with a knowing nod "... unlike that son of his."

"Now there's someone who could help out if he wanted to," Rachel said. "He made a fortune selling his mother-in-law's bungalow." She tossed her head in indignation. "Do you know how many houses they're squeezing on there?"

"I heard it was five," Daisy said. "Two four bedroom detached and some affordable housing."

"Surely that's Charlotte's money," Joan said.

Rachel shook her head. "He'll have it stashed away somewhere. She does whatever David tells her ... she always has. I'd like to see John telling *me* what to do."

"Men are so good with money," Joan said. "Fred sorts out all our bills on the computer."

"You could do it," Daisy said. "I'll show you if you like."

"Oh, I know how to do it but I like him to think I don't. It keeps him occupied now he's retired. He's always producing spreadsheets to show me how clever he is. I think it's quite sweet."

Daisy smiled at her. "That's very diplomatic. Can I sign you up? I think you'd be good on the committee."

"I'm not really a committee person, but I don't mind helping out behind the scenes."

"I suppose I could spare an hour to serve teas at the Craft Fair," Rachel said a little grudgingly. "Why are we calling it a 'Craft' fair? We always have a fair at Easter."

"It makes it sound better, different from usual. Right, well, I think we have a plan. At least I can show Fr. Jon we've made a start. I'll have to go across to the office for our meeting in a minute. Can someone tidy up for me?"

Rachel stared resolutely out of the window. Joan and Marion exchanged glances. "I'll do it," Vi said as she pushed her chair back and leant against the table for support. "There must be rain on the way my knees are giving me gyp. Drink up ladies; I want to get home before the heavens open."

CHAPTER 3

It was the first time Jon had tried one of the afternoon teas at Sue's Place. He seldom had time for such luxuries. Being the only incumbent in the parish his workload was vast; the organ was his first challenge, his second to petition for a curate.

The matching blue and white china sat well with the scalloped cloths and nineteen fifties decor. The cake plate, delivered by a willowy waitress in a frilly apron, was generously filled with bite-size offerings and as he savoured his first choice, a plain scone with a crunchy cheese topping and opened the newspaper he had picked up from the newsagent's next door, he wondered if his predecessor had been a fan of the cafe.

Father Robert Pryce had been nearing retirement and, from what he had gathered by talking to members of the congregation, not up for a fight over the organ. It had demanded all his innate ability in conflict resolution to help the Parochial Church Council reach a consensus. He guessed his success had been due in part to the gallons of tea he had drunk playing musical chairs with different combinations of parishioners ... and Marion Gray's rock buns, but that was only half the story.

Now the decision had been made, how to fund the project was the real problem. He had no experience in raising vast amounts of cash; could there be thousands waiting to be claimed from some obscure charity? He would have to ask Daisy to investigate. Sadly the money in a parish never stretched as far as people would like and with a bill for the new heating system as well as a substantial deposit for the organ falling due in the next few weeks, the situation had become urgent.

With all this going on in his mind he didn't see her walk in. It was only as he lowered the paper to tuck in to a rum baba that he became aware of her, seated at the window. He selected a slice of fruit cake. She was staring at nothing, the empty coffee cup her only companion. She had managed to squash her slight frame into the corner as if she wanted to take up as little space as possible; almost as if, he thought, willing herself to disappear altogether. He was trying not to stare at her but her face seemed familiar and he didn't want to make a faux pas so soon after his appointment by ignoring her.

He poured out another cup of the smoky brew and pretended to skim the headlines while he tried to work out where they had met before. Could she be a parish secretary ... one of the staff at the cathedral ... a deacon from another parish? The pages fluttered through his fingers like fivers at a fair as he moved from business to sport without reading a word and continued to take furtive peeks between mouthfuls of tea. She didn't look up as he rustled his paper and made a show of folding it away in a vain attempt to attract her attention. He watched as moments later she gathered up her coat and the parcel on the seat next to her and prepared to leave.

Shuffling out from behind the table he dragged the cloth with him tipping his empty tea-cup sideways into the saucer; he hastily re-set the china and only just managed to get to the door before her. "Don't I know you?" he said with what he hoped was a friendly smile. Her expression was blank. He held out his hand. "Jon Driver, St. Laurence's."

Her eyes skimmed the dog collar and then met his. The 'keep your distance' message was obvious; she ignored the hand. "I don't think so," she said volunteering no name.

He frowned. "I'm sorry. I thought we'd met before."

"I've probably got one of those faces," she said.

It was pale with delicate cheekbones, the blue eyes unreadable, half-hidden by fly-away hair; the brows finely drawn, fixed in a wary frown. He thought she had a look of Audrey Hepburn with her slight figure and generous mouth. He didn't hazard a guess as to her age. She seemed timeless, intriguing and, yes, attractive to him.

He glanced at the parcel. "Are you on the way to the post office?" he said hoping to prolong their conversation and feeling slightly foolish at the facile nature of his comment.

"Oh, this," she said, tucking the parcel more firmly under her arm. "It's for my son's birthday." She bent her chin at the same time lifting her shoulders to tip the hood of the parka over her head leaving her face in shadow. He found the child-like action both poignant and appealing. "Excuse me."

He stood aside to let her pass, the newspaper dangling from his fingers like the fan of an Edwardian lady, a frisson of disappointment tweaking his smile; she had a family and, most likely, a partner. He stared at her retreating form. For a minute he considered running after her and then checked the time on the old station clock over the till and knew that he couldn't. Daisy would be waiting for him.

Thyme let herself into the house and headed straight for the stairs. She had not counted on being remembered. Hauling down the loft ladder, she felt annoyed with herself for wanting to be. She did not need a man in her life, least of all a vicar. Since when had he been a vicar anyway? What did vicars know of real life cocooned in incense and buoyed up by their own platitudes; she had heard them judging others from their high moral thrones. It was easy to follow an ethical code when your life had not been challenged, but ... if she talked would he listen? There had been a minister once who had listened. He had tried to help ... strange that their names should be the same. She opened the suitcase and deposited the parcel inside. She dismissed the idea that they might be related as an unlikely coincidence and climbed down from the attic shutting the loft hatch with a bang.

"Thyme, are you there?"

Her brother's voice surprised her. She hesitated, wondering whether to respond or not. He must have heard her. There was no point in pretending he had not. "I'm here," she called.

Neil Sykes had the kind of face that no-one remembered; a perfectly acceptable face but an unremarkable one. His eyes were bog-standard blue, his hair a slightly receding bog-standard brown. His height was a bog-standard five foot ten, but there mediocrity ended. As a free-lance journalist he earned a comfortable living. He waited for her to appear in the hall. "You need to be careful," he said. "You left the front door open. Anyone could have walked in."

"It's just as well it was only you," she said.

He decided to let it go. "I come with news; do you want the good or the bad?"

"Hmm … let me think … the good news."

"We've done it. The flat's finally sold."

"That's great news … and the bad?"

"We've had to drop the price."

"I thought we might have to ... by how much?"

"Two thousand, but they've asked for a quick exchange. Next week, which means it won't be lying empty for months."

"That's ok."

"I was hoping you'd say that. I told the estate agent to go ahead. He's speaking to the purchasers tomorrow." He produced a bottle of Cava from under his coat. "We can celebrate at last."

She looked at him, her face full of fake optimism. She didn't feel like celebrating. She could pretend. Over the years she'd had ample opportunity. She would pretend, for him. "I'll get the glasses."

He poured out the wine and as she watched the bubbles subside she felt quite proud of herself. She hadn't broken down. He hadn't remembered. He hadn't noticed. She did not want him to notice, to know how she really felt today of all days. "That will be the last link, gone," she said.

"Yes, apart from Dad."

"He doesn't want to know. He couldn't even be bothered to come to the funeral ... his own sister's funeral," she said, her tone bitter.

"His floral tribute was impressive. What did you expect?"

"Nothing, I suppose."

"That's the way it's always been. We don't need him. He's always been more trouble than he's worth."

"Sad but true ... we'll have to sort out her stuff."

"I thought we could go over at the weekend."

"I'll make a start tomorrow."

"Are you sure you want to go alone?"

"Why shouldn't I?"

"I was thinking of all the memories."

"Only happy ones, Aunt Lal was very good to me."

"I know but it was your home for such a long time I thought it might upset you; isn't that why you moved out?"

"No. I wanted my own space. I never really liked living so high up. You don't seem to have any fresh air in a block of flats."

"Sure. So … what's been going on?"

"Nothing much," she said and then she remembered Jon Driver. "Well, nothing apart from the new vicar making a pass at me."

"You're joking."

"I'm not that bad looking."

"No, of course you're not. It's just … I ... um … I thought you weren't interested in men."

"Men are not generally interested in me, but I've had my

moments." Perhaps he hadn't remembered because he didn't know. She had always thought their mother must have told him.

"So, what did he say?"

"He said he thought he knew me from somewhere."

"Did he?"

She found a non-existent spillage on the chair and dabbed at it with a tissue. "No." It wasn't a complete lie. They had never spoken except for the usual niceties. She only knew his name because of the library ticket and he wasn't a vicar then. He did not know hers.

"There you are, then."

"There I am then what?" she said. "Just because I've never married doesn't mean I'm not attractive to men or might want a man in my life."

"No. Sorry. I'd forgotten. You were with Oliver Deans for a while."

He definitely did not know. She could not have told him. "That was years ago."

"What happened to him? He'd disappeared by the time I came back from France and Mum said not to mention it."

"That was typical of Mum. Brush it all under the carpet," she said a spark in her eye. "Never confront the issue, gloss it over and smell the roses."

"So, what happened?"

"It's ancient history."

"You don't want to talk about it."

She shrugged her shoulders. "He went off to uni. I went to London. We lost touch." The half-truth tripped off her tongue with ease. "Shouldn't you be getting back? Chantal will be wondering where you are."

"She's out with the girls."

"How long will it take for the money to come through?"

"It shouldn't be more than a few weeks if everything falls

into place, what are you going to do with yours?"

"I haven't really thought about it; Aunt Lal made me promise to give some money to the hospital ..."

"You'll be able to buy your own place now."

"I've kind of got used to renting. It has its advantages. I'm not responsible for leaky roofs or broken kettles ... how about you?"

"Chantal's got plans."

"I bet she has … expensive holiday?"

"Actually, no, she wants a new bathroom. Apparently ours is what they call 'tired'. Amy's been going on about riding lessons. The kit's pricey. Alice needs a new bike. She's really taken to cycling since Victoria Pendleton did so well at the Olympics. I'm sure we'll find something to do with it."

"I'm sure you will," she said.

The shutters were down. He felt the invisible screen every time he tried to build up a rapport. His sister revealed little of her private life. He knew he would get no more out of her now. They had been close at one time but that was years ago. Life and Chantal had intervened. His wife was ambitious. They had moved to suit her career, not his. He could work from home and be available for the children as and when they needed him.

It was lucky she had achieved the headship she wanted in a school near enough to Thyme for him to push for a house close by. He was a firm believer in the idea that families that played together, stayed together, but despite his best efforts Thyme did not seem to want to play. Chantal reckoned she must have been unlucky in love but he was not so sure. As far as he knew there had never been any serious relationships apart from Oliver.

He had thought that after their mother died they might have become closer but she didn't seem to want that either. Each time he suggested a get-together she backed out of it. She had been close to their aunt. Perhaps she was still grieving. He could understand that. It was five years since their mother had died and he still had moments of intense sadness. “I’d better go. I promised to get a take-away on the way back.”

“That reminds me, I’ve got some cakes for the girls. I was going to bring them round. You’ve saved me a journey.”

“What do you mean ‘cakes’?”

“I know Chantal likes you to eat healthily but you can’t have forgotten about cakes. Edible sponges topped with ooey gooey icing,” she said, “And *very* bad for you.”

He grinned. “Yes, I know about cakes; I’m just surprised you’ve been baking, that’s all.”

“I’ve been working at Quality Cakes all week. Jill had a wedding to cater for and Mr. Parks asked her to find someone to help Gemma in the shop. I was more in the bakery than the shop though. I enjoyed it. ” She stood up and took his glass, willing him to leave; wondering how much longer she could keep up the pretence.

“I didn’t know you were looking for a job.”

“I wasn’t.”

“It’s a bit different from the library.”

“They’ve closed so many I was unlikely to get another job as a librarian even if I’d wanted one and besides, I felt like a change. It’s only part-time.”

“Will we see you over the weekend?” She shook her head. “I’ll ring you when we’ve got a firm date for the exchange. We’ll both have to sign the contract.”

“Thanks, Neil.”

A brief smile flitted across her face as she went to fetch the cakes; it was a glimpse of the past, of the up-for-anything teenager she had been. There was no point in looking back. He wanted to move forward, make a future for them all together. He had no intention of giving up. He wanted to see that smile more often.

She returned with a white cardboard box dangling from spangled ribbon, ‘Quality Cakes’ printed on each side in purple lettering. “Thanks, I’m sure they’ll enjoy them. Speak soon.” She offered up a cheek for him to kiss and then added a hug before he left, clinging to him like a koala bear. “Come with me, the girls would love to see you.”

She shook her head. “No.” She wanted to throw him the ball of pain hoping he would catch it and she could be declared ‘out’ but that would be selfish and there would still be the walk of shame. She didn’t have the courage for that, doubted she ever would. The ball had to stay with her.

“What is it, Thyme?”

There was no way she could tell him. The smile was bright if insincere. “Nothing, I’m fine.” She had got used to lying. It was easier than telling the truth. “Give the girls a hug from me.”

CHAPTER 4

Jon tucked his scarf more snugly into his jacket. Daisy shivered. The calor gas stove in the corner of the parish office had barely raised the temperature above freezing. The windows were north-facing and the sun had gone down making it dark as well as cold. He switched on the light. "That's better. I really appreciate you staying the course, Daisy. The boiler should be repaired by the end of the week. I spoke to the heating engineer this morning."

"I'll be glad when February is over. Hopefully this will be the last winter we'll have to wrap up like Eskimos. The new heating system should be much more reliable," she said. "We've still got a way to go with the fund-raising. The organ will swallow most of it. We need another ten thousand at least."

"I haven't been able to think of any other ideas except applying for grants ... sorry."

"It's a good job Miss Barnes left us all that money otherwise we'd be sunk."

"We still have the book. My mother's rounded up all her friends to buy a copy but we need more takers."

"I wonder if she's tapped the Old Girls. I must ask her. I'll take the form in to work if you like; I'm calling in this week. I'll see if I can twist a few arms there," she said. "It's worth a try. I might have missed someone."

"I thought you were retired."

"I am but sometimes they need extra help, especially at the end of the tax year. I like to keep my hand in."

"You said something about a raffle."

"Marion and Bella will be doing most of the hard work. I just reel in donations from the local shops and there's one other thing," she said. "We're going to have a Craft Fair ... if you agree and the PCC have no objections; we always have some sort of fair around Easter. We thought we could make it more art-based this year. You'd be amazed how many local people have artistic skills."

"That's fantastic." He took in her eager eyes, the whippet-like face with its froth of white-blonde hair, the meticulously painted nails and wondered what he had done to merit such devotion from the PCC treasurer. "Saving the best till last," he said. "That's a really good idea. I can't see why anyone would object." She was his mother's friend but it wasn't just that. He felt that she wanted him to succeed in the parish on his own merit. He was glad of her help. He had been in post for such a short time that he relied on her for advice. He had noticed that the older ladies in the parish could not do enough for him. He was never short of a meal, some home-spun advice or a pair of helping hands. Perhaps the fact that he didn't have a wife had something to do with it. "That jar of coppers in the church is nearly full," he said. "That was a cracking idea. We must have emptied it twice already."

"Fr. Bob always had a jar 'on the boil' as he called it; it's amazing how much money you can raise in that way. People are glad to get rid of their loose change."

"Yes, he's a hard act to follow."

"No two priests are the same. I've known four since I moved into the parish and all as different as you could imagine. We were sorry when Desmond left, he was the one before last, but I think it was time for a change. We couldn't understand why he wanted to go all the way to New Zealand."

"I believe the countryside over there is fantastic. The climate's good."

"I know, but it's not England, is it?" Daisy said disdainfully.

"I saw those Maoris at Cardiff when they came over for the rugby; the faces on them ... they were worse than the gargoyles on the cathedral. I wouldn't want to meet one of them on a dark night."

"You're a rugby fan?"

"Not particularly. It's my boys, they're both dead keen."

"I didn't realise you had children nearby."

"I don't. They're my lodgers," she said. "They help pay the bills and make the house more lived in, I'd rattle around in there on my own. Have we finished now, father? I have to get back to do the evening meal. It's hotpot tonight. The lads love it."

"Lucky lads."

"You're welcome to join us."

"No, it's fine. I wasn't fishing for a meal. I'm cooking for my mother this evening. I think we've done all we need to for now, you go. I'm not staying much longer, myself."

She reached for her gloves. "How's the book coming on?"

"Slowly; I need at least thirty hours in every day to get it moving along. I guess this is my one act of rebellion coming home to roost."

"You mean choosing food over faith?"

"Pretty much ... I don't regret being a chef before I considered ordination but people do have certain expectations. It's a roast tonight, by the way, nothing exciting."

"You'll make someone a lovely husband ..."

"You're as bad as my mother. She's always telling me I need to get married."

"Every inspirational vicar needs a supportive wife," she said.

"I'm fine as I am thanks." He sensed her need to know more but he was not about to oblige. His private life was private and he planned to keep it that way. He knew how easily gossip could spread in a parish and besides, there was nothing to reveal.

"I've just had another idea."

"You're not planning to raffle me off are you?" he said.

"Not quite ... but how about auctioning your services as a chef, offer a slap-up meal to the highest bidder? You'd raise hundreds ..."

"I very much doubt it."

"... or ... we could have a parish supper in the church hall, cooked by you," she went on. "That could be a winner at ten pounds a head."

"When am I going to find the time for that? Thanks Daisy, but I think I'll stick to '*Holy Roasts*'. How many firm orders do we have?"

"It was a hundred and seventy at the last count."

He frowned. "I was hoping to have raised at least half of the two thousand by now ... that's my goal. I think it's achievable."

"The numbers are building slowly and steadily; I'm sure we'll get more takers as time goes on. You haven't done that interview I arranged for you on local radio yet. That will help." She pulled the beanie hat over her ears and eyebrows, leaving hazel eyes just room enough to gleam at him above the toggles as she fastened the collar of her duffel coat round her chin. "You could become a national treasure."

"With you on side, how can I fail? Thanks Daisy, see you on Sunday."

"Indeed you will. Send my love to your Mum. Tell her I'll give her a ring about the Old Girls. We've got a re-union coming up. I haven't kept in touch with as many as I should have, but between us we should be able to contact quite a few and persuade them to buy your book. We could invite them to a book signing or something although it's a long way for them to travel just for that."

"Perhaps they could make a weekend of it. Linchester is worth a visit with the cathedral and the Merchant's House."

“We’ll call it a book launch, that sounds suitably swanky ... we could offer wine and nibbles. They’d be here in a flash if we mention wine and you never know who has a birthday coming up; the book’s an ideal gift ...”

“You don’t need to give me the hard sell, I’m writing it,” he said.

“It *would* make an excellent gift, though.”

“That reminds me talking of gifts ... I met someone at Sue’s Place.”

“Most people meet at Sue’s Place eventually.”

“No, I mean someone I haven’t seen round here before ... a stranger.”

“So, there’s a stranger in town,” she said in a gun-slinging tone, raising two fingers pistol-style in the air as she blew smoke from the make-believe barrel.

“She might not be a stranger to you. I’m new here, don’t forget ...”

“She?” she said, her eyes alight with expectation.

“Don’t get excited she’s probably married. She certainly has a family. It was her son’s birthday.”

“How old was she?”

“At a guess I’d say, late thirties ... thin; sad eyes. She looked sort of awkward sitting there, you know, uncomfortable ... as if she’d rather not have been there at all.”

“That’s not much to go on.”

“I’ve developed an antenna for troubled souls. I’d love to know her story.”

“Haven’t you got enough on your plate?”

“Probably ... I can’t help wondering, though. It goes with the territory.”

“Scrub what I said before,” she said with a wry smile. “Every inspirational vicar needs an *uncomplicated* wife. She was probably sorting out party bags in her head. I’d concentrate on the book if I were you. I’ll keep you posted about the committee."

"Owen will be upset if you don't ask him."

"I know. If we could persuade one of the other men to join us it might help."

"I'm happy to pop in and out. I want to do my bit but I can't commit to being available for all the meetings. Try Bella's husband. Doesn't he have a Punch and Judy? We might be able to rope him in for a performance."

"I hadn't thought of Ben. He knows everyone from his post office days. The Punch and Judy would fit in perfectly with the craft theme. It will encourage all the young families to come. Pester power will draw them in," she said. "I'll pop over and see him. Well, time to love you and leave you."

"Let me know how you get on with Ben," he called. She acknowledged his comment with a backward wave as the door swung behind her.

He locked up the office and walked the few yards over to the vicarage wondering whether everything would meet his mother's exacting standards. Mrs. Ram had been over the house thoroughly. He had noticed the shiny taps in the bathroom. He had stocked up the fridge himself. She always checked that. Surely he had thought of everything. What did it matter if he hadn't? He appreciated her advice on parish matters ... he respected the fact that she had played the part of rector's wife to perfection. She never complained when he picked her brains if he was stuck on a message he wanted to get across to his flock ... but she still kept an eye on his domestic arrangements as if he had only just left home and he didn't need it. "I'm back, Pan," he called. A moth-eaten moggy appeared at the kitchen door, mouthing a silent welcome. Her eyes were not as sharp as they had been; her legs more uncertain.

He shrugged off his jacket and unwound the scarf, dangling them both from the newel post. He strode off into the kitchen lingering by the door for a moment and then about-turned to put the jacket and scarf away in the hall cupboard; he had been taught that there was a place for everything and that everything should be in its place. He grinned, pulled the jacket from the cupboard and draped it back over the newel post. "Man, not mouse, Pandora," he said. "Let's get cooking."

Thyme tipped the rest of the wine into her glass and put the bottle in the re-cycling bin. She watched the bubbles dance and then took a sip, gulping the rest down like a dose of bad medicine. How was she to bear the empty months ahead with her chief confidante gone? Aunt Lal had understood. She had been there. She couldn't talk to Neil. She wasn't close to Chantal. Jill was not the sort of friend you could open your heart to unless you wanted the whole world to know. And then there was the vicar. Perhaps Jon Driver would listen. Perhaps she could rely on him to keep quiet. It was part of their moral code. He would be obliged to keep her confidence if she asked him to hear her confession. He might refuse to do that. After their encounter at Sue's Place she could not blame him ... no, he was a vicar. It's what vicars did. He would have to help if he were asked.

She left the glass on the draining board and headed for the stairs. Taking the baton from its corner in the airing cupboard she fished for the catch on the loft hatch and prised it open. The ladder sprung down to settle firmly on the landing carpet with a twang as the spring stretched into place. Grasping the wooden hand rail she stepped onto the first rung and then the next until she was swallowed by the darkness above.

CHAPTER 5

Chantal Sykes swung her legs free of the steering wheel and inched out of the driving seat of her Mazda MX5. She stretched her torso slinky-style to scoop up her coat and bag from the passenger seat and then clicked open the boot as she walked round to the back of the car. She bent her neatly cropped head over the mountain of A4 paper and lever arch files to extricate two. Tucking her iPad under her elbow, she crooked her arm to nurse the files and quickly incarcerated the rest before walking briskly towards the house. “I’m home,” she called.

Neil appeared as she dumped the files on the dining room table with a weary sigh. “I asked the girls to go round to the shop for some bread. My ordering system seems to have let me down. How was your day?”

“Hectic as usual ... I’ve got a pile of work to do this evening,” she said. “When are we eating?”

“Ten minutes.”

“What have you been up to today ... did you finish that article?”

“Nearly ... I called round to see Thyme this afternoon. Guess where she was when I arrived.”

She crunched her brow, ice blue eyes noting his concern. “I haven’t a clue.”

“She was in the attic.”

“The attic ... what was she doing up there?”

“I didn’t like to ask. I’m worried about her. She’s been acting really ... well ... odd lately.”

“How do you mean?”

"As if there's something she's not telling us."

"She doesn't have to tell you everything. There are bound to be things she wants to keep to herself."

"I know but I get the impression she wants me to know something but doesn't want to say it, if that makes sense."

"It's probably part of the grieving process. Is she coming at the weekend?"

"No."

She stroked his arm. "Would you like me to have a word with her?"

"I doubt it would help."

"It might; you could just be too close. She might open up to me. That counselling course the governors ran at school was very useful. I've been able to sort out several traumas with the children I wouldn't have known how to handle before ... shh ... I think the girls are back," she said as the front door slammed.

"We'll talk about it later," he said.

Alice sauntered through to the kitchen. "Dad, Amy is weird," she said and then she noticed he wasn't there. "Da – ad," she yelled.

"No need to shout, we're in the dining room," he said

She appeared in the doorway, childhood lingering where maturity was struggling to settle. The proportions were all wrong. The slender frame too tall, the face too small, the teeth too large; nothing had arrived where it was destined to be. "Hi Mum ... Amy is completely crazy," she said. "She's going on about flies now."

Amy pushed past and went to stand beside her mother. "I was just saying it was strange how flies can get into a house through the tiniest of spaces but can't get out even if you open the door for them," she said.

Chantal put an arm around her shoulders and smiled at Neil over her head. "That's very true ... it's what you call original thinking. It's not weird at all, Alice."

"Anyone who's interested in flies is definitely a weirdo," Alice said and flounced off to her room.

Diana Driver parked the car and crunched up the drive to her front door. She let herself into the flat; the flat she and Andrew had chosen for their retirement. She was glad they had not moved far from the old parish, it avoided the need to make new friendships. The faces in the shops were still well-known to her and their favourite walks within easy reach. Even the postman was the same. That familiarity had been a godsend in the bleak months immediately following his death.

She kicked off her shoes in the small square hall and passed down the magnolia-tinted passageway lined with family photographs through to the kitchen, dumping her bag on the nearest worktop. She thought it was a blessing her son could cook. It would avoid the influx of maiden ladies in the parish who tended to hang around a vicarage kitchen if there were no other females to fill that space.

Andrew had never been able to see their ministrations as a threat to their marriage ... but then he had been a bachelor for years and he loved his food. He had refused to turn away any of the offerings brought to the rectory door in Tupperware boxes, ice cream tubs, or someone else's best china. She had been more sceptical of their motives.

With teabags and apples filed away she went into the bedroom to stow the 'get one free' soap powder under the wardrobe and bemoan the loss of her old-fashioned rectory. It might have been draughty but at least it had plenty of room for storage. When Andrew retired they had spread the larger pieces of furniture amongst various family members before they moved into the flat. Her niece had taken most of it. Cath had a large home in Yorkshire filled by her large family. She had embraced the farming lifestyle. Six children was a lot to cope with but she seemed to flourish in the chaotic household and still had time to administer a couple of holiday lets and entertain her favourite aunt several times a year. She was grateful for that. She knew Jon couldn't do it. The life of a vicar in a busy parish did not leave much time for entertaining elderly relatives.

She had been very happy with Andrew despite the twenty year age gap. Jon was like him in many ways and she had not been surprised when he finally bowed to the inevitable and chose a life in the church. Stubbornness was not such a bad thing, she mused. It was sometimes necessary in the successful running of a parish. There were always different factions with their own agendas; someone had to rein them in without fear or favour and then try to unite them.

She contemplated her son's career choices and decided that being in charge of a kitchen was not a million miles from being in charge of a parish. It was as important to understand the characteristics of each of his parishioners as it was to understand the ingredients in a recipe; each one was necessary to enhance the flavour and build the mix. It would be unwise to allow the stronger ones to overpower the weak. Mistakes with the quantities could result in disaster. The trick was to get them all working together.

She smiled as she remembered Andrew saying, "In any church the whole is always greater than the sum of its parts ..." He had delivered that nugget of insight over tea and biscuits in the covered cloisters after Jon's ordination. She recalled how he had insisted on walking through the doors of the cathedral for the service. She had helped him from his wheelchair and watched his shoulders stiffen with pride as he saw his son parade up the aisle with the other ordinands "... and if you remember that, son, you won't go far wrong. Aristotle had a marvellous way of putting things."

She sat on the bed and took one of the cushions lying there, cuddling it to her like a soft toy as she felt tears well up. If only they had managed another few years together. Another few years of his wisdom and his warmth ... but it was not to be.

He had made her promise to find another partner after he had gone. He knew she would miss him and that time would hang heavy on her hands without a husband to fuss over but she wasn't ready. She did not want to contemplate committing to another long-term relationship. The promise had been made because he had been so insistent and she had wanted him to be at peace in his final hours but she knew in her heart that it was unlikely to happen.

She had tried to keep herself busy. Life after Andrew was not the same, but it was bearable. It was already better with Jon moving so near. She guessed it would just be the two of them that evening. The last thing she wanted was to be a burden to him. She tried not to interfere in his life but sometimes she could not resist passing on helpful hints. Now she was greedy for his company and if she was honest, keen to sample his cooking again. No-one produced puddings like Jon did. She was hoping for Tiramisu.

CHAPTER 6

Several large potatoes lay on the chopping board like beached whales. He sliced them into wedges and tossed them into a saucepan of boiling water as he tried to remember where he had seen her before. He had a good memory as a rule. Faces were no problem; names were more of a challenge. If he thought hard enough he reckoned it might come back to him. He glanced down at the cat smirking at him with half-open eyes. "Who is she, Pan? What's her name, what's her story? ... Anna ... Debbie ... does she look like a Debbie? Oh sorry, you didn't see her, did you? I think she's more of a Florence or an Emma." The cat purred, vibrating gently against the cupboard. "She might have been a customer at one of the restaurants. She could be a runner ... she's got the build for that ... slim athletic ... I think you'd like her. I like her. She said she didn't know me. Was she lying? No ... why would she do that?"

And yet, in the back of his mind there was a persistent niggle, a sense that he did know her and that she knew him. He reckoned if he stopped trying, perhaps it would come back to him. He put the potatoes in the oven with the chicken and glanced back at the cat. She was watching him sphinx-like, her pale eyes flecked with amber. "Don't go getting any ideas," he said as he shut the oven door with a snap and set the timer. "You've already had yours." She miaowed plaintively and rubbed her arched body against his leg. He picked her up and stroked the sparse fur, his hands tracing her bony spine as he remembered how well-covered it had once been and the silkiness of her crow black back. "We've got half an hour before dragon o'clock," he said. "That's just time for a wind-down glass of wine."

The cat ambled out of the room anticipating his next move. He poured out the wine and headed for the sitting room furnished with a mixture of his mother's cast-offs and a brand new sofa with marshmallow cushions deep enough to accommodate his long legs. He drew the heavy curtains and flipped on the brass lamp with its nubile dancer propping up the umbrella shade. The phone rang as he let his back relax into the cushions in the mellow light. He put the glass down with a sigh and sat up to listen as the answer phone kicked in.

"I need to have a word about flowers." He recognised Nuala Cooke's Scottish accent. "I'll call back tomorrow."

No action necessary. He let his body curve into the feathers again and rested his feet on the coffee table. The cat jumped onto him purring like a tractor. She pummelled his lap with soft paws turning every so often to find a place to settle and then melted into his knees. "Don't make yourself too comfortable, I'm getting up again soon," he said as he stroked her head. They stayed like that until the doorbell rang and he encouraged her onto the floor. Her cushioned paws slid along the carpet and she glared at him before stalking off into the kitchen. "I did warn you," he said as he made his way to the door.

Diana Driver kissed her son's cheek and handed over the bottle of wine she had brought with her.

"Merlot, thanks."

"Your father always enjoyed a glass of red."

"I remember."

She untied the paisley scarf she had wrapped about her shoulders and handed it to him. The years had been kind to her. Her shoulder-length hair was streaked with grey but still abundant. Her eyes were bright, her skin clear, almost unlined and her figure trim. "Who were you talking to, do we have company?"

He tossed the scarf over his coat. "It was only Pandora."

"Where is she?"

"She went into the kitchen."

The cat was sitting on the floor near the oven, a quizzical expression on her feline features, her tail tucked neatly over her paws. She gave half a miaow in welcome but remained with her back leaning on the warm cupboard.

Diana smiled. "She seems to have settled well. Where have you put her box?"

"It's under the table." As if she understood them, the cat unwound herself, stood up, stretched her paws out in front of her and walked slowly towards the table, tail held aloft like the rolled umbrella of a tour guide.

Diana bent down to fondle her ears. "Has he been feeding you? I know what he's like when his mind's on other things." Another purr rattled round the cat's throat. She picked her up and rested her over one arm, at the same time languorously stroking her back.

"You don't need to worry about that," he said. "I think she's put on weight. Half the parish feeds her titbits. Mrs. Ram's her biggest fan."

She deposited the cat in the wooden box and watched her settle down in the folds of the crocheted blanket, tucking her head down and curling her tail round her body like cotton round a reel. "She looks so comfy."

"She spends more and more time sleeping these days."

"She's doing very well for her age. Can I do anything to help?"

"No, I'm just about there. Take a seat, madam." He draped a tea towel over his arm and escorted her round to the other side of the table. "Excuse me while I serve up," he said.

Diana peered under the table to watch Pandora snoring gently and twitching in her sleep. "It's amazing how her fur has stayed so black considering her age. She's a funny cat."

"She mooched about the house like a lost soul until I

unpacked the box. It's taken a bit of a battering after all our moves but she'd never forgive me if I threw it away."

"Hopefully you won't be moving again for a while. It should see her out."

"She's sixteen now."

"Yes, she's quite an old lady. Betsy's still got Delilah. It must have been a good litter. Did I tell you she wants me to go on a painting holiday with her? Goodness knows why. I enjoy my dabbling but I've never been much good at art."

"I expect that's why she invited you. She knows you won't outshine her efforts," he said approaching the table with two generously filled plates.

"That's a bit cynical ... I thought it was because she thought it might be fun and she fancied some sibling bonding. This looks good. I'm not sure I'll be able to get through all those potatoes," she said regarding the crispy mound with a doubtful eye.

"Don't worry. Pandora and her friends will polish off the leftovers."

"You don't leave food outside, do you?"

"Yes ... why?"

"Rats," she said wrinkling her nose at the thought.

"They're all God's creatures, isn't that what Dad would have said?"

"He never had a very practical outlook on life, bless him. You'll end up with foxes in the back garden if you're not careful. How's the fund raising going?"

"We're still a bit short. Have you had any more genius ideas, anything that doesn't involve me feeding the five thousand? Daisy seems to think I can run a parish and have time for everything else too. Sadly I'm not Super Rev."

"You could auction one of my works of art," she said trying to needle him into criticism of her talents.

"I meant any *sensible* ideas."

"Well how about a Dutch auction. I've still got a whole load of clutter you could have. I'm sure you could persuade Tom Briggs to do the auction for nothing ... or an auction of promises."

"They're both good ideas. I'll have to run them past the fund-raising committee. Apparently the ladies are organising a craft fair over Easter and a raffle."

"I'll donate something to that. Jumble sales can raise the cash but it's difficult to get volunteers to help with the sorting and selling … I bumped into Ria at the supermarket last week. I haven't seen her for years. She was always great with sorting jumble. She was buying cat food. Apparently she runs a cat rescue centre now."

"She was always cat mad … emphasis on the mad."

Diana frowned. "She would have made you a good wife."

"I don't think so. We weren't right for each other."

"I just want to see you settled."

"I am settled. I'm very happy as I am. I don't have the time to devote to a relationship, not at the moment anyway."

His mother gave him an old-fashioned look. "It's been a long time since Lucy. I'm sure if the right girl came along you'd find the time."

"Lucy and I wanted different things; if we hadn't parted when we did, it would have happened another few months along the line. I wish you wouldn't keep on about me getting married. You're as bad as Daisy."

"How *is* Daisy?"

"She sends her love; still keeping me in order and making sure the parish finances are up to scratch; I didn't know she took in lodgers."

"She's been doing it for years, ever since Adam died and Rebecca moved to Canada. Strange that, your daughter is supposed to be your daughter for the rest of your life and of course your son is your son until he takes him a …."

"Don't say it," he said menacingly.

She wrinkled her brow in resignation. "I must give her a ring. There's a big school reunion in June. I thought we might go together. It's great being back in touch again."

"She mentioned it. She thought we could invite your Old Girls to the book launch, tempt them with wine and get them to part with some cash ... we need to boost the orders somehow."

"It's certainly an idea ... how are you getting on with the writing?"

"Not as well as I'd like. I've enough recipes just not the big chunks of time I need to set them out on paper ... but I have a cunning plan. I'm due some time off. I plan to spend it finishing the book."

"There are still several months to go. I'm sure you'll do it. You just need a little …"

"... application ..."

She smiled at him, a fond, proud smile. "I was going to say, trust in your own ability. Wait a minute ... I've just thought of something. Do you remember that painting Dad bought me years ago ... the one of the dogs?"

"I thought you gave it to Cath."

"No, I couldn't bear to part with it then ... too many memories but I haven't an inch of wall to hang it on. I'd rather turn it into an organ."

"Are you sure?"

"I am and anyway, it's an Isobel Flynn. I read somewhere that her early works are quite popular. It could raise a big chunk for you."

"Tom will know. I think they have two auctions a month now. They're doing very well by all accounts."

"I'll take it over tomorrow, see what he thinks."

CHAPTER 7

Diana knew where the painting was. She had stored it on the top of her wardrobe, along with the Scrabble board and an old mirror that had belonged to her mother-in-law. She liked the mirror. It was shaped like a church window, the frame decorated with silver and brass repoussé work featuring exotic birds perching beak to beak. She was determined to find a suitable space for that, but for the moment it had to stay where it was, cushioned in bubble-wrap for safe-keeping.

She set off the next day with the painting in a canvas bag, hoping to find Tom Briggs at the sale room and not out and about.

Upfordham was a pleasant village with its flint cottages and narrow streets surrounded by rolling countryside. It had flourished over the years. The boundaries had seeped southwards towards Linchester with the luxury housing scheme and a new shopping mall. There had been two pubs in the village at one time; the Bandy Goose, with its hard core of regulars due to the skittle alley and successful darts team, had survived. The Unicorn had morphed into a co-op. Property prices had soared. She felt sorry for the young people who had grown up there but could not afford to get a toe on the property ladder. Most of them had moved into Linchester where there was a flourishing rental market and houses were a more reasonable price.

Due to the burgeoning real estate side of the business, Reedman & Briggs' sale rooms had re-located to a small business park to the north of the village not far from her old home in the parish of St. Giles. The cedar-boarded building had weathered into the countryside and, surrounded by silver birch and willow trees did not look out of place with the fields of oil seed rape.

She could see a modern reception area through the glass doors. There was a desk either side of the foyer and a couple of easy chairs, a coffee table between them loaded with magazines. As the doors opened in front of her, the two receptionists looked up from their screens; an older woman with unnaturally dark hair gelled away from heavily-made up eyes and the other young, mousy and fresh-faced. "How can we help?" said the older of the two.

"Is Tom about?"

"He is," she said as the phone rang. "You take it, Amber." She fingered the designer glasses lying on the desk in front of her as if, Diana thought, she expected there to be a problem and then satisfied that Amber could cope, she turned back to her. "Sorry, you wanted Tom?"

"I need him to value something for me."

She picked up the phone and tapped out a number, silver bangles jangling. "Tom ... could you come over please ... someone in reception to see you." She smiled at Diana as she put the handset down. "He'll be right over. Take a seat."

Diana sat down in one of the easy chairs and rested the bag on the floor beside her, gazing at the photographs of successfully auctioned lots plastered to the walls like exam results.

"Diana ... this is a surprise. It's good to see you again." His voice startled her with its depth and familiarity. She turned away from the picture of a valuable Chinese urn to be greeted by a Kaffe Fasset needlepoint waistcoat and a shock of unruly hair, dark, abundant, resting like a canopy over his thickly-fringed eyes. The clean-shaven chin was firm and the smile genuine as he approached her. She stood up to accept his embrace and was surprised at how good it felt. She was at first reluctant to remove herself from his arms until she remembered they weren't Andrew's. She stepped back quickly and covered her embarrassment with a smile. "Tom, it's good to see *you* again."

"What brings you all the way out here?"

"I'd like you to value something for me," she said, lifting up her bag for inspection.

"Do you have time for a coffee?"

"Why not ..."

"Excellent. Two coffees please, Amber," he said. "Come on through. How's Jon? I keep meaning to give him a ring."

"He's the reason I'm here. The church needs a new organ and a new heating system. I'm afraid Bob Pryce let things slide. How's your mother? I haven't seen her at NWR recently."

"She hasn't been well," he said, a tight smile urging his expression to soften but not quite reaching the dove-grey eyes. "Alzheimer's."

She caught her breath. "I am *so* sorry. I didn't know. You must be devastated."

"It's just one of those things. She didn't want anyone to know when it was diagnosed. We've tried to keep everything as normal as possible ..." he was interrupted by a knock on the door and Amber appeared with two mugs on a tray. "Thanks," he said briefly.

"You're welcome," she said flashing him a smile as she left.

"I feel a bit of a nuisance now," Diana said. "You've got enough on your plate without this."

"Not at all ... work's the only thing that's keeping me going."

"Can I do anything to help?"

"We're managing all right. She has a carer now and the children have been very good. I'm sure she'd like a visit, though, if you have the time. She loves to reminisce about the old days. It seems to calm her down. What did you want me to see?"

She reached into her bag. "It's this painting; I haven't a clue what it is worth. Andrew bought it for me years ago. I want you to sell it and whatever it raises I'll give to Jon for the new organ."

He cast a critical eye over the little oil painting. "Dogs are always a popular subject," he said. "And no-one does them better than Isobel Flynn. I've got several clients who are big fans. We sold one of her watercolours of the Lakes here last month. It went for six thousand. I don't think this is in the same league but it's still good. Possibly two ... how does that sound?"

"I didn't expect it to be worth that much. Jon will be delighted."

"Are you sure you want to part with it if Andrew bought it for you?"

"I don't have anywhere to hang it in my tiny place and he was the one who loved dogs. I'm more of a cat person."

"What about a reserve?"

"I don't know. I want it to raise as much money as possible. What do you suggest?"

"Well, you don't want to give it away. It's a good cause; I'll mention it at the auction. Let's say fifteen hundred."

"I'm happy with that."

"Good. I'll do my best to squeeze out as much money as I can."

"Thank you ... look ... I would like to visit your mum. When would be the best time?"

"Any time, she doesn't go out now. She wouldn't be able to find her way home if she did," he shook his head hopelessly. "Just give me a ring first. Some days are better than others."

"It must be so hard for you, and for the children. I know they were close to their Gran."

"It's worse for her. The medication has stopped working and she's changed so much. Everything scares her. The carer does her best but Mum gets nervous if I'm not there. Things get put away in the wrong places and then she forgets where they are. She was such a neat person it really upsets her."

"I can imagine."

"I'm torn between wanting to go to work and wanting to be there for her. She's always been there for me, especially after Janine left. I dread the day when she doesn't know who I am. It's not very pleasant watching your mother turn into someone you don't know any more. Some of her friends can't deal with it."

"I'm free tomorrow. I'll call first thing to make sure she's up to it."

He gripped her hand as she got up to leave. "That's really kind of you, Diana; I appreciate it. I'll tell her you're coming."

"Will she remember?"

"Probably not but it keeps up the pretence of normality for me."

"Does Jon know she's ill?"

He shook his head. "I keep hoping she's not as bad as she is. I don't like talking about it. I don't know why I'm telling you."

"I'm glad you have."

"Mum was always so independent. She never asked anyone for help, even after Dad died. I feel as if I'm letting her down discussing her affairs with other people."

"She's not who she was any more. She needs help and you can't do it on your own. From what I know of Mary, she would understand." She eased her hand gently from his grasp and patted his arm. "I'll see you tomorrow."

CHAPTER 8

Morning prayers were over. Jon checked for messages on the answer-phone in the parish office hoping to find nothing too urgent or taxing that required his attention. He was planning to sneak some editing into his day if he could.

His mind escaped for a moment as he reclined in his chair, feet resting on an old kneeler he had rescued from the store cupboard, wondering if they might meet again ... hoping they would. He tried out more names, mouthing them under his breath in an effort to solve the puzzle of her identity, when the door burst open and cracked against the wall rebounding into Daisy's shoulder as she stood, white-faced on the step.

He could see she was shaking as he scrambled to his feet, sending his chair skittering into the filing cabinet. "Whatever's the matter?" he said. "You look awful."

"There's been an accident," she said, wincing from the blow and rubbing her shoulder. "She just walked out in front of the car ... I saw her do it ..."

"Who did?"

"I don't know."

"What do you mean?"

"I don't know her."

"Is she badly hurt?" Daisy nodded. "Have you called an ambulance?" he said, patting his trousers, searching for his mobile phone.

"Yes, yes ...please hurry. We need a blanket or something to cover her, it's bitter out there ... the dust sheets, they'll do," she said.

"Dust sheets?"

"The ones we use to wrap the statues in lent. They're in one of those drawers," she said, waving a wild arm in the direction of the built-in wall unit alongside the window. "The driver's sitting in the road."

"How fast was he going?"

"Not fast at all but he couldn't have avoided her even if he'd been going at a snail's pace ... she just walked out in front of him ... she bounced, literally bounced off his bonnet."

"He's probably in shock."

"It wasn't his fault ... how could someone do that, I mean deliberately walk out in front of a car?"

"Is she conscious?"

"No."

"You'd better go back and stay with her. The ambulance won't be long."

"The police might arrive first."

"I'll be with you in a minute," he said, already rifling through the deep mahogany drawers. The dust sheets were in the last one he tried; clean and neatly folded like towels in an airing cupboard. He grabbed a few and raced outside to join her.

The woman was lying in the road, one of her legs bent at a strange angle. From what he could see of her skin it was very pale; her features masked by a tangle of hair. A thin trickle of blood oozed from her forehead. Daisy was kneeling in the road at her side trying to stem the flow with a tea towel. "Do you think I should put her in the recovery position?"

"No, leave her. She may have hurt her neck ... or her back. Here, I found them," he said handing over the bundle he had brought with him.

"Thanks." She covered the woman with several layers and then stood up. "That's better," she said. "I wish the ambulance would hurry."

"I think I can hear it." He squatted down to get a better look at the casualty, squinting through the matted hair. He lifted a few blood-soaked strands from her forehead and then recoiled and leapt to his feet. “It’s her ... it’s the woman I told you about yesterday, the one I saw at *Sue’s Place.*”

“The stranger, you mean?” Daisy knelt on the pavement to have another look at the unconscious face. “I saw her, too. She was at church when I arrived for tea and chat.

“Who is she, Daisy ... what’s she doing here?”

“I really don’t know. I can’t imagine what would make someone do something like that.”

“She might not have done it on purpose. She could have tripped or something we need to find out her name.” He scanned the nearby pavement. “Did she have a bag with her?”

“No ... just a box of cakes. They’re squashed.” She pointed to the box lying on its side in the road, the cardboard collapsed like a fallen kite. It was close to the wheels of the car, which had been abandoned where it had swerved to avoid her. The driver’s door was open; skid marks clearly visible in the road. “I thought I’d better not touch them in case the police need them for evidence or something.”

“She said it was her son’s birthday.”

“I remember you telling me. The cakes must have been for him.”

“At last ... here they are. We’d better get out of the way,” he said. They stood back against the fence as the ambulance drew up, lights flashing and siren howling. “You tell them what happened, Daisy. I’ll go and see if I can help the driver.”

The man was sitting on the pavement as Daisy had said, his shaven head clasped in his hands, his whole body juddering. He didn’t get up as Jon approached. “Are you ok?”

“I don’t know. I can’t stop shaking.”

“The police will be here in a minute.”

“It wasn’t my fault. I couldn’t do anything. She just stepped off the pavement in front of me. It was such a shock. One minute I'm singing along to my Abba tape and then ... bang ... just like that."

"A cup of tea ... let me get you a cup of tea."

"I can still hear the thud. I hope she's not dead."

"No ... she's still alive. The ambulance people know what they're doing. She's in good hands ... tea?" He shook his head. "Perhaps one of the paramedics should look you over."

The man suddenly got to his feet. "No ... no it's fine, I'm all right. I have to get off to work."

"At least have a word with them. You may not be fit to drive. You still look a bit shaky to me. The parish office is only over the road. I could phone your work and explain what's happened while you rest in there. The heating's on the blink but it's warmer in there than it is out here."

"I'll be all right. I'll go and sit in the car for a bit before I set off. I need to call my wife."

"The police will want your details."

"I'll give them to you. Will pass them on?"

She was drifting in and out of consciousness. Conversations were going on, in and around her head. She couldn't tell reality from fantasy. She wasn't in pain. She was floating above everything, looking down from a great height.

"How long has he been in Scotland?"

"He was at university up there. He decided to stay."

"What's he doing?"

"He's a training instructor with the mountain rescue."

"Don't you worry about him?

"He knows those mountains like the back of his hand. He wouldn't take any chances."

"What's his name?"

One of the paramedics was fiddling with a blood pressure

monitor. "What's her name?"

Jon shook his head. "We don't know. We don't even know if she lives locally. She's not one of my regular parishioners."

"Matthew, I call him Matt."

"It's a shame he's so far away. I don't suppose you see him much. I can't imagine not seeing my kids."

"We keep in touch. He's very good about all that. I'm planning a trip up there in the summer. He said to go in June before the midges get too bad."

"Her injuries are quite bad. We've stabilised her but we need to get her to the hospital as soon as possible."

"What's the damage?"

"Broken leg, concussion ... could be some internal bleeding. We can't say for sure until she's been x-rayed."

"I'll come with you."

"I can go if you like," Daisy said. "I'm free today."

"It's fine. I'll do it. Could you track down the bakery? They might know who she is."

"Of course; I'll do that and meet you at the hospital."

"I'd better get back or the Wobbly man will be after me."

"You'll call him that to his face one of these days."

"I don't know why his wife doesn't put him on a diet. She is a nurse you know."

"Is she?"

"Yes, up at the hospital. She was there when I went in to have Teale. Do you like it here?"

"The hours suit me. I don't want to work full time. I don't need to really. My aunt left me some money."

"Lucky you, I don't have a choice. I hope you do stay. It's nice to have someone to chat with over lunch."

"Thanks, Gemma. I'd better get back, too. She'll be ready

for the next batch by now."

The painkillers were wearing off as the ambulance screeched to a halt in the hospital car park. The paramedics unloaded the stretcher and she was back. She saw lights flashing behind closed lids. She groaned. A nurse took her hand. "Hello ... you're in hospital ... can you remember what happened?"

"The cakes ..." she mumbled.

"You've been in an accident ... you're in hospital," she said louder and more clearly as if talking to someone with impaired hearing. Thyme opened her eyes and then closed them again. "What's your name?"

"It's Thyme," she whispered. She was a ball of pain, deep, throbbing, unbearable pain. It hurt to breathe; her ribs ached; her head was thudding but her leg was even worse. She wondered how much more she could take. She wanted the pain to stop. She couldn't think, only feel ... her face contorted in an effort to deal with it.

"I'll give you something for the pain," the nurse said. "She's not with it," she whispered to Jon who was standing beside the bed, waiting. "People talk all sorts of nonsense when they're in shock and they've had morphine. We'll have to get her details later." She bent over Thyme's head. "I'm going to top up the morphine and then we'll send you for an x-ray.

The lights faded. The voices were silenced and then there was nothing.

CHAPTER 9

Ben Jeffers saw everything from his eyrie. The witch's hat turret adorning the modest semi and the one on its twin were ideal look-outs over the town; one to the east and one to the west. They had all the attributes of a double folly. No-one could remember why the two houses had been designed in that way, or even who had been the architect of such frivolity but it was a constant worry that one day they might topple over and bring the two houses crashing down with them. They were known by the locals as 'the twin towers' and a useful reference point for strangers being only a stone's throw from the church and the source of the meandering river Syme.

He saw everything but said nothing. He said nothing but kept a note of everything he saw. A not so spritely seventy, he tended his allotment when it suited him, played dominoes in the Bandy Goose and had learned over the years how to deal with his wife's indolence. He did most of the shopping on-line but he liked to get meat fresh from the butcher's in the village. He kept the house clean by means of a strict rota while she reclined on the sofa with her poodle, Mimi, watching the shopping channels or dipping into the latest chick lit whilst munching a never-ending supply of crisps.

Bella Jeffers was happy with this state of affairs. Ben was resigned to it. He had known her for ever but it was only after her first marriage ended tragically that he had taken on the ready-made family. He loved Bella. He loved his step-son. He was hoping that one day he could persuade her to get on a plane so that they could visit him in New Zealand. They hadn't met his partner. He wondered what would happen if a wedding was on the cards. He wondered if she would step outside Upfordham if grandchildren started arriving. Skype calls were all very well but you couldn't hold a baby in your arms through a computer screen. Up until now she seemed content to live her life from a couch but he was biding his time.

He had seen the accident. He had seen Jon Driver get into the ambulance with the casualty and he had seen Daisy Parsloe hop onto her bike and pedal away. "Bella," he yelled at the top of his voice as he tumbled down the last few stairs in his desperate need to get to the bottom. He picked himself up and rubbed his coccyx. "Bella ... there's been an accident by the church."

Mimi yapped and jumped off the sofa. Bella opened her hooded eyes a fraction wider and tipped the last few crumbs of salt and vinegar down her throat. "What?"

He panted out the words again. "There's ... been ... an accident."

"How do you mean?"

"Hit and run ... or was it? I don't think it *was* an accident."

"Was it that new vicar?"

"No, it was Thyme."

The colour drained from her face as she turned towards him.

"Thyme Sykes?" He nodded vigorously. "It can't be."

"She's back, Bella and she didn't look too clever."

He was sitting, waiting, praying with his head in his hands and no nearer to working out where he had seen her before. He still did not know her name. He wished Daisy would hurry up. She might have news. He was just thinking about another cup of tea when through his contemplative fingers he caught sight of a duffle coat and then Daisy's high-heeled boots. He sat up straight and returned her smile.

"Is there any news? How is she?" she said as she clacked down the corridor towards him. "I bought you a sandwich."

He shook his head. "Thanks ... nothing ... I don't know. They took her off for an x-ray. They've been gone ages. Did you find out who she is?"

"Thyme Sykes and she's not a stranger. The family lived round here years ago. I vaguely remember the mother."

"It's an odd name."

"From what I recall the mother was a bit odd ... into all this new age stuff. Her husband ran off with a Spanish dancer. Thyme's been working at Quality Cakes. Jill Dobson knows her quite well. She's coming in as soon as she can."

"So she's a baker, then."

"No, a librarian, she was just helping out as and when. Her aunt was a solicitor in Linchester. She died and left her a fortune, that's why she's back here, renting a house in the village because they're selling the flat. She doesn't really need to work."

"What about her son?"

"We were wrong about him. He's grown up; lives in Scotland apparently. Works for the mountain rescue."

"So she's on her own."

"Yes, well, there's a brother. I don't know what happened to him. Her mother died years ago. You need to ask your mum. She must have had dealings with them ... aha ... there's someone coming."

"It's the nurse who admitted her," he said.

Walking towards them with a firm tread, the rubber soles of her shoes squelching along the polished floor was a tall woman of Nordic appearance. "She's in theatre," she said addressing Jon with piercing blue eyes. "Ruptured spleen; the head injury isn't serious but it'll need monitoring; one of her legs is quite a mess. They might have to pin it. I think she'll be in for a while. Have you found out who she is? We really need to call someone for her ... let them know she's here."

"We've got a name," he said. "Thyme Sykes."

"Time?" she said her head cocked at an angle like an inquisitive terrier.

"As in parsley, sage and rosemary," Daisy said. "She works at the bakery in Upfordham. Her friend's on the way in. She'll let the family know."

"Good. I'll update her records. There's not much point you waiting now. She's likely to be in theatre for another hour at least. Why don't you come back tomorrow?"

"That's probably best," Daisy said. "Now Jill knows, she'll sort out everything."

"You'll tell her we were here," he said. "I don't want her to think no-one cares."

"I'll see someone tells her."

"I expect the police will want to interview her."

"They won't be doing that for the next twenty-four hours. She'll be too groggy for questioning," she said.

"I'm sure that can wait," Daisy said. "I saw the accident. They can ask me anything they need to know for the moment."

"What did happen?"

"She was just standing there, all on her own, as if she was waiting for a bus or something but we haven't had a bus in the village for years," she said. "I was just about to ask her if she was lost when I heard a car coming. She stepped out into the road and then ... it happened. That poor man; I wonder how he is."

"Did he come in here?" the nurse said.

"He wouldn't. He said he was ok. He left his details with me and I gave them to the police," Jon said.

"I told them it wasn't his fault," Daisy said. "There was nothing he could have done to avoid her."

"I said he shouldn't drive until he felt less shaky but he just wanted to get off to work," Jon said. "I can't believe she did it on purpose. I hope they manage to contact her son."

"It's amazing the lengths they go to when they want to trace someone," the nurse said. "They'll find him."

Neil Sykes was on a deadline. Everyone seemed to think being free-lance was a sinecure. They should try being on a deadline, he thought. Tossing another tight ball of crumpled paper into the bin, he heard the back door slam.

"Dad ..."

"I'm in the office, Amy."

Footsteps raced up the stairs. "Have you seen my tennis racket? Jade's mum's waiting in the car."

"I thought you took it to school with you this morning."

"I took my tennis bag but the racket wasn't inside."

"Try the garage."

"I already have."

He sighed, untangled his legs and pushed his chair back from the desk. "Right, I'll come and have a look."

"I bet Alice has taken it."

He glanced at his daughter's crumpled shirt, the sleeves of her school jumper frayed at the edges where she had sucked the wool instead of her thumb and the halo of curls that his mother used to say made her look like the image of Princess Anne on the green savings stamps she had collected as a child. He noticed her scuffed shoes. "What on earth have you been doing? I cleaned those shoes last night."

"P.E.," she said. "I forgot my trainers." She smiled up at him, the smile transforming her face, making a dimple appear in either cheek.

"The smile that launched a thousand ships," he said.

"Helen of Troy," she retorted.

"You won't be allowed to forget things when you go to big school," he said. She had always been one for literature rather than sport. The tennis lessons were a sop to her mother and although he knew the child enjoyed the exercise, he also knew her heart was not in it. He caught the hint of a rubber encased handle peeping out from under the duvet which had half-slipped from her bed. He reached down and pulled it out, throwing the duvet back into place at the same time. “One tennis racket,” he said.

She reached up on tiptoes to kiss him briefly. “Yuck. You need a shave,” she said and then she was gone, out of the room, down the stairs and through the front door like a wraith, leaving a solitary, “Bye,” floating in the air behind her.

He returned to his desk and tried to pick up from where he had left off. He soon realised there was nothing to pick up on; the screen was empty. He knew he would get nowhere now he had been interrupted; his inspiration had lapsed like a neglected gym membership. He clicked on his emails, deleted some spam and decided a shot of caffeine might help.

The house was still a work in progress. Chantal wanted a shiny new bathroom with a slipper bath, twin sinks and a generous shower cubicle to match the new kitchen they had arranged before moving in two years previously. Getting the tiling finished in the kitchen had been a nightmare from start to finish and he didn’t relish the thought of another tussle with Darren Morgan. Deciding on the tiles, waiting for replacements for the ones he had cracked and working their way round his numerous days off, meant the job had taken months rather than weeks.

Being self-employed himself, he had not been able to understand how Darren managed to make any money at all, the pace at which he worked, but he had to admit it had been worth the wait.

He thought Chantal’s vision of the bathroom sounded like the screen set from a Hollywood blockbuster. She had decreed mirrored walls, polished black tiles and shiny chrome fittings. Goodness knows how long Darren would take with all that.

He poured boiling water onto the coffee grounds in the stainless steel jug and fitted the plunger neatly over the aromatic scum. The phone rang as he waited for it to brew. “Ye-uh-lo.”

“It’s Jill Dobson.”

It was a moment before he registered who she was; Thyme’s friend. “Oh, hi Jill, what can I do for you?”

“It’s not good news, I’m afraid. There’s been an accident. Thyme’s in hospital.”

He felt the blood drain from his face; his legs trembled as he sank onto one of the bar stools for which Chantal had spent hours trawling the net. “What happened?”

“She was run over outside St. Laurence’s.”

“Run over ... is she alright?”

“A broken leg and concussion, I believe.”

Relief left him light-headed. He let more air filter into his lungs. She wasn’t dead. She wouldn’t be paralysed or brain damaged as he had feared in his original panic at hearing the news. “Where is she?”

“St. Peter’s; I’m on my way there now.”

“I’ll come as soon as I can. I need to work out what to do with the children first. Thanks for letting me know.”

CHAPTER 10

Ben was not surprised when he saw Marion on the doorstep that evening. “I thought you might be round,” he said. “Come in, I’m just brewing up.”

“How is she?” she asked.

He shrugged. “You know your sister. She’s not saying much.”

“Is she in there?” she said inclining her head towards the front room whilst at the same time handing him her coat.

He nodded. “I’ll be with you in a mo.”

It was uncomfortably warm in the room. Bella was reclining on the sofa, floral clips in her blonde hair, a crimson kaftan attached to her body like the petals of a tropical bloom. The dress strained to accommodate her matronly stomach and chunky knees as she leaned across to pick up the remote and flip off the television. Mimi yapped but stayed on her lap as her sister approached the sofa. Bella made no attempt to get up. Her shapely legs were stretched out on the cushions, her surprisingly slim toes bare, the nails glittered with polish. “What do *you* want?” she said.

“I’ve come to see if you are all right.”

“Why wouldn’t I be?”

“I heard about Thyme.”

“I suppose everyone’s talking about it.”

“I don’t think many people know. I only found out because Hilary Dobson came over to show me Jill’s birthday cake. Thyme’s been working at the bakery.”

“Why did she have to come back?”

“Her roots are here.”

"I don't know how she has the nerve to show her face."

"She did what she thought was best at the time. You can't blame her for that."

Bella's eyes flashed. "I can and I do," she said.

"They were barely more than children. Oliver was just as much to blame."

"Don't bring him into it. She had him wrapped round her little finger. She did a terrible thing. She deserves to suffer."

"Bella, that's an awful thing to say. You should have forgiven her by now."

Bella's eyes were bathed in tears. "I'll never forgive her. She took him away from me. Ollie wouldn't have ended up on the other side of the world if it hadn't been for her. Why did she have to do it?"

"It was the wrong time for them."

"They were going to be married."

"You weren't exactly over the moon about it."

"Oh, so now it's my fault, is it?"

"That's not what I'm saying. I just think you're being unfair."

"Ollie was devastated, that's why he went away."

"That wasn't what he told me."

"Are you saying I don't know my own son?"

Marion sighed. "There's no point raking over old coals," she said. "What happened ... happened. It was very sad but it wasn't all down to Thyme and it was a very long time ago."

"Not a day goes by when I don't remember everything as if it were yesterday. She ruined my life."

"Here we are," Ben said as he edged his way into the room with a tray. "Here's a nice cup of tea. Anyone want a biscuit?"

Jon had decided not to wait until the morning. He had telephoned the hospital and had been told that Thyme was 'comfortable'. That was an improvement. She could not have been described as comfortable when he had last seen her. He buzzed into the ward. “Father Jon Driver. I’m here to see Thyme Sykes.”

“Come in. She’s in bay three.”

He walked up the polished corridor, peeping into the other bays as he passed. Most of the beds were full, the occupants finishing their supper snack. A trolley clanked on its way to collect the empties helped along by a smiling Philippino girl in a simple red and white striped dress and soft-soled shoes. She stopped to have a word with each of the patients before taking their cups and plates and moving on to the next one.

Thyme did not have anything on her tray. She seemed to be asleep. One of her arms was attached to a drip and her head was resting on two pillows, her eyes closed. Her slim form hardly made an impression under the tightly tucked bedding. He sat down beside her. “Hello again,” he said. She did not move. “I still haven’t remembered where we met but I know your name now, it’s Thyme. That’s very unusual.”

He wondered if she could hear him. “We’ve been in touch with your friend Jill. Has she been in to see you?” There was no response. “We’re trying to get some money together to replace the organ at St. Laurence’s. Daisy, she’s our Treasurer, said that you visited us recently; perhaps you heard the old one. It is pretty dire. It’s going to take us ages to get all the money together but we have a fund raising committee now so I’m hopeful we’ll make inroads on it soon. We’ve already paid the deposit. We need to put up one of those thermometer boards so that everyone knows how we’re doing.”

That idea had just occurred to him but he reckoned it was a good one. Any publicity was surely good publicity. People passing the church would see at a glance why they needed money. He would speak to Daisy about it ... or Owen ... perhaps Owen was the right person. Having a job to do would prevent him from causing too much mayhem for the fair organisers. “I’ve only been in Upfordham for a few months but I know the area quite well. I grew up round here. Someone said you used to live here. I wonder if we met then. Did you go to the High School in Linchester? Perhaps that’s why I remember you.”

He couldn’t think of anything else to say. He crossed his legs and listened to the monitor bleeping. He watched the screen and noted her blood pressure change and then the regular rhythm of her heart. His eyes wandered over to her face, to the eyelids decorated with dainty blue veins; purple bruising spread out from the boundaries of the bandage encircling her head, down her cheek onto her neck. Someone had parted her hair in the middle. It looked all wrong combed either side of her face. He admired the symmetry of her lips; the hands lying on the white bedspread, un-ringed, unvarnished, unmoving; like the alabaster hands of a saint.

“I can’t stay much longer,” he said. “Don’t worry about your son. Don’t worry about anything; just concentrate on getting better.” He watched her for another few minutes and then stood up to go. “I’ll be back again tomorrow.” He wanted to kiss the tempting curve of her cheek, to squeeze her hand. He wanted to sit there until she woke up but he knew he could not.

He moved out of the bay. As the curtains were drawn right back he had a clear view of her bed as he walked towards the entrance to the ward, turning several times, hoping to see some change in her. He stopped by the nurse’s station. A doctor was sitting there, her hair tied back in a ponytail, a stethoscope tucked round her collar, sleeves rolled back as she checked an x-ray. She looked up at him. “Jon Driver,” he said. “St. Laurence’s; I’ve just been to sit with Thyme Sykes.”

“She’s still under sedation. Her body’s taken quite a battering but we are happy with her progress, no cause for concern. She should be more awake tomorrow.”

"Right ... thanks. I'll call in again."

Neil stared at his sister's comatose features. What had she been thinking? The constant bleeping of the machine beside the bed grated on his ears. He wished he could switch it off and yet he was scared it would stop at any minute; flat-line and then that would be that. He gripped his hands together and willed her to open her eyes and then he reached out to touch her cheek. It was pleasantly warm. He was surprised to realise that she had a look of Alice as she lay there. He had never noticed it before. He felt two hands on his shoulders and glanced up into his wife's face.

"I got here as soon as I could," Chantal said. "How is she?"

"There's been no change," he said troubled eyes meeting hers. "Why did she do it Charne?"

"It might have been an accident."

"I knew there was something wrong. I told you there was. I should have made her admit it."

"It's not your fault it happened."

"I was in a hurry to get the takeaway. If I'd stayed longer she might have opened up to me."

"Well now we know there's a problem we'll be able to help," she said.

"What did you tell the girls?"

"I just said she had been run over crossing the road. I didn't want them to get the wrong idea. Nobody really knows what happened. We'll just have to wait until she wakes up. Do you want a coffee? "

He shook his head. "I had some water earlier."

"I'm having one or I'll fall asleep. I've had a shocking day."

"You don't have to stay with me."

"I want to." She brushed his forehead with her lips. "We'll find a doctor before we go and see when she can come home. She needs proper food to make a quick recovery and she's unlikely to get a decent meal in here."

"She won't be able to manage the stairs at her house."

"I don't think she should be on her own anyway, not at first. She can stay with us. I'll make up a bed in the dining room."

"Thanks, Charne," he said. He sighed. "I wish I knew what was going on in her head."

"Not a lot at the moment," she said. "She's sleeping very peacefully. Sleep is what she needs now. It will do her good. I'm going to find that coffee. I won't be long. You think nice thoughts for her while I'm away."

He stood up and walked round the other side of the bed to where a chair rested under the naked window. He stared out into the night, his eyes drawn to the shadowy hospital outbuildings, metal grills attached to the windows like braces on uneven teeth. A row of giant bins was lined up against a wall, crisp packets flapping against their wheels in the blustery wind. His gaze roamed further afield to see street lights twinkling in the distance. He could hear the faint roar of traffic and some muffled music coming from a pub across the road. Life carried on. Why would his sister have wanted to end hers? She had friends, family; no money worries. He struggled to understand; he did not want to understand her motives if she had walked out in front of the car on purpose. He wanted to believe it was an unfortunate accident but he couldn't be sure. He turned towards the bed and gazed down at her. "Why, Thyme?" he said softly, "Why?"

"What are you going to do about it?" Marion said. "You ought to do something."

"Why should I?"

"Well, I would if it was me."

"I don't want to have anything to do with her," Bella said. She selected a bourbon cream from the plate of biscuits Ben had provided for their refreshment and divided it into two, licking the filling off one finger of the biscuit before nibbling at the rest like a rabbit with a carrot.

Marion and Ben exchanged glances. “Come on, love,” he said.

“Come on ... what?”

“She was nearly your daughter-in-law. The accident practically happened on your doorstep. Are you going to tell Ollie about it?”

“He won’t want to know.”

“We could call the hospital, see how she is,” Marion said.

“No,” Bella said.

“I might send her a card,” Marion said. “It will be a while before she can walk properly again. Hilary said Jill told her they had to pin the leg and there were internal injuries.”

Bella straightened her back, her jaw like a set-square as she fixed her sister with a steely glare. “You do what you like. I’m doing nothing.”

“She might have died,” Marion said.

“It’s a pity she didn’t,” Bella said.

“You don’t mean that,” Ben said. “I know you don’t.”

“You don’t know anything,” Bella said bitterly.

“I could speak to Fr Jon,” Marion said. “He will know how she is.”

“I think you should,” Ben said. “He’s a nice lad. *You* should have a word with him, Bella ... Bella?”

She raised her brimming eyes to his, Mimi licking salty tears from her cheeks. “We never see him on his birthday. It’s too far for him to pop in for lunch. We don’t know anything about his life now. I’ve lost my son because of her.”

“Ollie wanted that job,” Marion said. “It had nothing to do with Thyme.”

“He wouldn’t have gone if they’d stayed together,” she said.

“You could go and visit him.”

“We could, Bella,” Ben said. “He keeps asking us to go.”

"I wouldn't have to go all the way over there if he was still here. He *would* still be here if she hadn't spoiled everything. I'd have had grandchildren if they'd stayed together. It's all down to her. I don't care if she never walks again. I don't care if she lives or dies."

The telephone was ringing as Jon let himself into the vicarage. He walked into the study and flipped on the Angle Poise lamp, dropping his keys on the desk as he shrugged off his leather jacket and picked up the phone. "Fr. Jon," he said crisply.

"It's me," Diana said. "I've been to see Tom Briggs. Good news about the dogs."

"What dogs?"

"The painting ... Isobel Flynn, remember?"

"Oh yes," he said. "Sorry, there's been a lot going on."

"You sound fed up."

"I've just come back from the hospital. There was an accident outside church today."

"What sort of an accident?"

"A pretty serious one ... someone got run over."

"Who was it?"

"A woman ... Thyme Sykes ... Daisy said you might know her."

"Thyme ... yes, I remember her. I thought she was in London. How bad is it?"

"Bad enough ... she's had quite a knock on the head; one of her legs is broken and there are some internal injuries."

"What a nightmare ... poor girl. How did it happen?"

"Daisy seems to think she did it on purpose."

"Surely not ... there are easier ways."

"What can you tell me about the family? She said there was a brother."

"Yes, Neil. He moved back here about two years ago ...

funnily enough I bumped into him in the supermarket last week; his wife's head at the Barnes Academy. They're in one of the houses by the golf course. She must have been visiting them."

"No, she's renting a place in the village. Her aunt died recently. They're in the process of selling her flat."

"I didn't know she'd died ... are you ok?"

"It was a bit of a shock to be honest. I saw her in Sue's Place the other day. It was strange. She looked familiar but I couldn't place her. I suppose I must have remembered her from way back."

"She can't have been more than ten when you went off to do your chef's training ... those children had an unconventional up-bringing. I'm glad they seem to have come through it without any lasting damage."

"I'm not so sure. Maybe she does have problems. It could have been deliberate. Anyway I won't know what I can do to help, or even if she needs my help, until we've had a proper chat. She was still under sedation when I went in to see her."

"She'll be alright though."

"Physically, in time; mentally, who knows? I can't do any more for her tonight. What did Tom say about the painting?"

"He reckons it should do well. I've left it with him. He has his own issues. Mary's ill."

"Is it serious?"

"Alzheimer's. He's struggling. I said I'd tell you. He could do with a friendly ear."

"That's really sad. She was always so full of life."

"Apparently several of her friends have deserted her. They can't deal with the way she is now."

"It must be difficult."

"Life can't always be fun, Jon ... let's face it, quite often it isn't."

"I'll put him on my list."

CHAPTER 11

Two magpies cackled from a chimney-pot as Jon set off to visit Thyme the next morning. A good omen if he believed in such things. One piece of good luck he acknowledged was that, being a priest, he could be admitted to the wards any time he liked.

A cleaner was mopping the floor when he reached the ward her plastic apron crackling as she worked. Some of the bays were shrouded in curtains but the ones round Thyme's bed were still pulled back. She was awake, propped up on pillows and although her cheeks were pale she looked much brighter.

As he walked down the ward she saw him and smiled. "You look better this morning," he said.

"I seem to have caused everyone a whole load of trouble."

"May I sit down?" She nodded. He dragged one of the chairs nearer the bed. "We were all worried about you."

"I'm sorry," she said.

"It doesn't matter. You're on the mend which is good. How's the leg?"

"Sore."

"What happened?"

"I don't know. One minute I was waiting to cross the road and the next ... I woke up in hospital," she said. "I didn't do it on purpose, if that's what you think."

"I wasn't thinking anything," he said. "I'd decided to wait until we had a chance to talk."

She pulled a face. "They've already sent a psychiatrist to see me."

"I think they have to if they suspect you're suicidal."

"I'm not."

"No ... we didn't get off to a very good start, did we?" he said.

"I'm sorry about that, too. I was coming to apologise for being so short with you," she said. "I'd taken cakes."

"I thought they were for your son. You said it was his birthday."

"He's in Scotland," she said.

"Do you want me to let him know what's happened?"

"He already knows."

"We had met before," he said.

"In London," she said.

"London? No. I was talking years ago. You went to the youth club at St. Giles. My father was rector there."

"I thought the name was familiar; I don't remember you from then," she said. "I remember you coming into the library where I worked in London."

There was a pause while he searched for the same memory. "Yes, of course ... the Carnegie Library."

"You weren't the Reverend Jon Driver, then."

"I was a chef."

"I didn't expect you to remember me."

"I'm usually quite good with faces."

She stared out of the window and he felt her withdrawing. "Daisy, our treasurer, she saw the accident, she said you came to the church the day before. Is there anything I can do for you?" He adopted a jokey tone. "I do a nice line in weddings ..." she plucked at the sheet tucked round her waist as he continued "... confirmations, baptisms ..."

"I thought it might help ... being there."

"And did it?"

She shook her head. "I've done some things I'm not proud of."

"Nobody's perfect," he said. "Talk to me."

"It's complicated," she said.

"It's always complicated." There was a flurry of activity in the ward; a posse of students was on its way round and he reckoned she wouldn't be prepared to say more with an audience. It was important to him that she did say more. He wanted her to trust him. It didn't matter how much he tried to pretend otherwise, he felt drawn towards her. "We can't talk now. I'd better go. Give me your address. I'll come and see you when you've been discharged."

"They haven't told me how long I'll be in here. I won't be at home for a few days after that either. I'm staying with my brother."

"We can meet there."

"I don't know."

He pulled a card from his wallet. "Look, I want to help ... here's my number. Call me when you're ready."

She smiled; it was a pathetic wobble of the mouth and no more than a watery crinkling of the eyes. He wished he could stay longer. "Thanks," she said.

"See you," he said. As he walked down the ward and negotiated his way through the labyrinth of hospital corridors he wondered what she could have done that had affected her so badly. He was surprised at the strength of his emotions. Offering her counsel was going to be a challenge but he couldn't allow his feelings to cloud his judgment ... perhaps it was already too late; he was involved and he was going to have to deal with it.

"Daisy," Diana said.

"Diana," Daisy replied and then backed away from Diana's embrace. "No, don't come too close I think I might be coming down with a cold."

"That's a nuisance."

"It is, especially when I'm so busy. One of the lads has been sneezing all over the house and it's been so cold in church without the heating; it's hardly surprising."

"Well, come in," she said. "Here, let me take your coat."

Daisy unfastened the toggles of her duffel coat and handed it over to Diana after extricating a large wad of tissues from the pocket. "I love this place," she said. "It's so homely."

"It doesn't feel like home to me."

"I can't believe we were living within a few miles of each other and I didn't know you were there."

"It's too easy to lose touch with people."

"I remember that," she said walking over to an enormous vase standing on the floor against the only bare piece of wall in the room. "It was your grandmother's."

"It's awful, isn't it, but somehow I can't bear to part with it."

"I haven't much left from the old days. Josie auctioned the whole lot after my parents died."

"Wasn't there anything you wanted?"

"I wasn't asked and being the youngest I would have been outvoted anyway. We all got a share of the money." She sat down and glanced around the rest of the sitting room, her eyes alighting on the photograph of Andrew Driver. "I expect it seems strange being here on your own."

"A bit ... I wish we hadn't moved in such a hurry. I would have liked a garden. I am glad Jon's nearer now. How's he getting on?"

"He's made a big hit in the parish. All the old dears love him. Doesn't Rachel Meeks live in this block?"

"Rachel and John, yes. They're in the penthouse. Are they friends of yours?"

"She goes to St. Laurence's. We never see him."

"I think he's abroad a lot. I don't really socialise with the neighbours apart from passing the time of day when I see one or other of them in town. If we had a communal hall I might get to meet them more."

"Jon's really getting his teeth into the organ project. It's about time something was done about it. We're reduced to the clapped out piano from the vestry now which is a complete embarrassment."

"He said you'd ordered the new organ."

"We had a bequest which will cover most of the cost but there's still a huge hole in the budget," Daisy said.

"I'm donating a painting Andrew bought me. Tom Briggs is dealing with it."

"It's such a shame about Mary. She was in our bridge club."

"I went to see her this morning."

"Did she recognise you?"

"She did but it was awkward to know what to talk about and she kept repeating herself."

"It must be difficult for Tom. I feel so sorry for him."

"I said I'd go again. What more can any of us do?"

"Nothing; it's the one thing I dread, losing my marbles," Daisy said fielding a sneeze.

"Me too," Diana said.

"I know he can escape when he goes to work, but it's still there waiting for him when he goes home."

"She has a carer now. Things won't ever be the same for him ..."

"... or her ..."

"No, but they're managing. Will you come to the auction with me ... Jon doesn't know if he'll be free or not."

"I'd like that. Let me know when and where. If it's in the morning we could have lunch afterwards to celebrate."

"I'm getting worried now that it won't sell; it's a good painting, but you never know."

"I'm sure it will make the money. People love dogs. I wanted to talk to you about fund-raising. Do you think we could have a book launch and round up some of the Old

Girls?" Daisy said. "They might buy a few copies."

"We could mention it at the re-union dinner."

"We need to do something before June."

"We'll have to send out a round robin. I'd offer to host it here, but there's no room."

"We'll do it at my house. It's more central anyway."

"Don't you live in the Tasker's old house?"

"That's right ... we were lucky to get it. They sell like hot cakes in Cooper's Close. Maggie Watt's house has only been on the market two weeks and she's had five viewings already. It's in a terrible mess, hasn't been decorated for years."

"It sounds like a good project for someone."

"They're welcome to it. It's not just the house, the garden's completely overgrown. Come over for coffee. We'll sort out the details of the book launch and you'll see what I mean. We'll fix a day before I go. Did Jon tell you about the accident?"

"Thyme Sykes you mean, yes; what a shock. How's she doing?"

"She'll be ok. She's a very lucky girl."

"She was a serious little thing. Kate had to bring up Neil and Thyme on her own you know. Their father was hopeless; money just slipped through his fingers, never held down a job for more than a few months and he always had an eye for a pretty face. Kate was very attractive."

"I think I remember her ... vaguely. Thyme's not bad looking. She's a bit battered at the moment though."

"She would be. I think Kate did some modelling for a while. Andrew married them. We all hoped it would encourage Mark to be more responsible, settle down, but as soon as the children arrived and she had to spend more time with them, he didn't like it."

"Men don't."

"They had some awful rows. Andrew tried to mediate on

several occasions but it was a waste of time. Eventually they split up and Mark skipped off to Spain."

"What about the aunt? Didn't she have money?"

"Harriet was completely different. She was a solicitor in Linchester. She did her best to give them all some stability. I think Thyme lived with her for a while. Kate drifted away from the church. She got into all this new age stuff, crystals and sleeping under the stars. She was always going off to festivals in her campervan, sometimes for weeks on end, taking the children with her whether it was the school holidays or not."

"She'd be fined if she did that now."

"She needed to be a free spirit."

"There must have been gypsy blood somewhere in that family."

"I don't know about that. I do know they rented a cottage down by the Syme. As they got older the children looked after each other. They had such an erratic upbringing I'm surprised they both did so well. They missed an awful lot of school."

"I've always been drawn to home education. Briar Lodge was like a prison camp."

"It wasn't that bad. The food was ok."

"Are we talking about the same school?"

Diana laughed. "You didn't taste my mother's cooking."

"What happened to the brother?"

"He went in for journalism. He's back here again, too. I bumped into him at the supermarket the other day. I got to know them when they came to the youth club Ben and Bella helped set up at St. Giles. Andrew was keen for the young people to have somewhere to go and their son was a teenager at the time. It turned out to be very popular."

"Ben often mentions Ollie. He's in New Zealand now."

"I think he was a bit of a handful. I couldn't understand what Thyme saw in him. They were teenage sweethearts, you know ... inseparable until he went to uni and she went off to

London."

"Jon thinks she needs his help. I told him he shouldn't get involved but he seems determined."

"You won't get him to change his mind, Daisy. He might be able to help. I hope he can. I've always had a soft spot for Thyme."

"I really ought to go now," Daisy said. "My head's banging."

"Can I get you something for it?"

"No, I'll be fine ... I'll give you a bell about that coffee."

"There's no hurry. You look after yourself."

"If I don't, no-one else will," Daisy said with a wry smile.

"I know ... it is a bit like that when you're on your own ... if you need anything call me. I'll fetch your coat."

CHAPTER 12

Ben never felt the cold. A few days later when he walked across the road to the vicarage he was coat-less, his shirt sleeves unbuttoned, rolled up to expose wrinkled elbows. His arms swayed to and fro like elephants' trunks, fists clenching and unclenching with every step. He had hitched up his trousers when he left the house but as his hips rolled, they inched slowly downwards until his shirt parted company with his trousers to reveal generous folds of flesh encircling his waist.

Nuala Deans was in church watering the flowers and tidying up dead leaves and stalky off-cuts when he opened the door and ambled in. "Have you seen the vicar?" he said.

"Uh huh ... he's in the office."

"Do you think he'd mind if I disturbed him?"

"I shouldn't think so. You'll know if he's busy. The door will be closed."

"Ok, thanks."

The door was open. He could see the calor gas stove Owen had sourced to make working in the parish office a little more bearable. It made him think of the paraffin heater his father had used to take the chill off his workshop. He'd inherited the Punch and Judy skills from him, the steadfast attitude and almost unending patience. "Morning vicar," he said. He hitched up his trousers again as he shambled in. "You'll be glad when they get that heating fixed."

"I will indeed," Jon said as he un-tugged the scarf still swaddling his neck and hung it on the back of his chair. "It's good to see you, Ben ... take a seat. Are you here about the committee?"

"No. I wanted to have a word about Bella."

"What's up with Bella?"

"It's a long story. I should have done something about it before but, well, you know how it is," he said, his shoulders drooping. "And now all this bitterness is eating her up."

"Bitterness ... that's not good."

"It started years ago. Now Thyme's back, everything's come to a head."

"You know Thyme?"

"Yes ... she should have stayed away." Jon walked across to shut the door. "She was engaged to be married to Bella's son, Ollie."

"Go on."

"They were in love, you see. Bella wasn't happy but he wouldn't listen. Thyme was only eighteen but he was twenty and always knew his own mind. He was her only son. I don't suppose anyone would have been good enough to be honest. I liked Thyme but I didn't dare say so. She wasn't like the other girls, always twittering on about something or other ... but he wasn't my son, what could I do? He and Bella came to me as a job lot, so to speak. I always feel as if I'm treading on eggshells where Ollie's concerned."

"I see."

"They split up and he went to New Zealand."

"I don't understand the problem here."

"Bella thinks he went because Thyme broke his heart. It broke her heart, too. She hasn't been the same since. He never came back and now here's Thyme's to drag it all out in the open again."

"Does Bella know you're here?"

He shuffled uneasily in his seat. "No."

"What do you think I can do to help?"

"Try and make her see sense ... talk to her. She won't listen to me."

Neil's expression was harsh. "I still don't understand. Why on earth did you do it?"

She could almost see him wagging a finger at her. "I wish you'd stop asking me that. I didn't do it on purpose."

"Do you expect me to believe you? I knew something was up. I would have helped. You know I would." He glanced about him in a furtive manner and lowered his voice. "You didn't have to do anything silly."

"What have you told the girls?"

"I said it was an accident."

"It *was* an accident, just an accident. I didn't see the car."

"You must have heard it. How could you not have seen it?"

"I had loads going on in my head. I was planning to go over to the flat ..."

"So what were you doing by the church?"

"I wanted to see the vicar."

"Why?"

"I thought talking to him might help." She avoided his gaze. "I guess I'm still upset after Aunt Lal."

"None of this makes sense. There's something else, I know there is."

"Honestly, there isn't."

"I wish I could believe you."

"You could if you wanted to."

"Why were you really there?"

There was no way she was going to tell him the truth. She wanted to salvage some sort of a relationship with him. "I was wondering what I should do with all that money if you must know. I thought I might donate some to the church. They need a new organ. I walked into the road without thinking; I forgot the green cross code," she said hoping to raise a smile. "It was a stupid thing to do. I'm sorry I worried everyone. What with you, the vicar and the psychiatrist I'm beginning to think you all want me to believe I did it deliberately but I didn't."

"Ok, fine ... if you say so ... anyway, Chantal's sorted out a bed for you in the dining room. You can stay with us for as long as you like."

"I'm feeling much better today. I haven't seen the doctor yet but I'm hoping to be discharged soon."

"Your vicar's been in touch."

"He's not *my* vicar. What did he want?"

"Nothing really, just to see if he could do anything to help. I think he feels responsible because it happened on his patch."

"He's Andrew Driver's son."

"I know. Here, have a grape."

"Why does everyone always think they have to bring grapes?" she said as she contemplated the generous bagful on offer.

"You like grapes, don't you?"

"I do but a bottle of wine would have gone down better."

"You'll have to wait for that. Can I bring you anything else?"

"Smoked salmon?" she said.

He laughed; she joined him and then stopped abruptly to clutch at her stomach. "Don't make me laugh, it still hurts."

"How's the leg?"

"It's not too bad. I'm getting the hang of the crutches."

"I reckon they'll be chucking you out soon."

"I hope so. I'd rather be anywhere else but here."

Jon could see the old man was struggling. "I won't tell her you've been here if that's what you're worried about. Anything you say will be between us ... in complete confidence," he said.

"It's not that. I'll tell her myself when I get home. I just don't know which way to turn. You see, she thinks Thyme drove him away. He told us they'd split up when he came home from university. Bella was over the moon until he said he'd accepted a job in New Zealand. Thyme was still in London working as a librarian. They were supposed to be saving up for a wedding so it all came out of the blue. It's not just that she blames Thyme for him going ... she blames her for everything that's wrong in her life. It's eating her up."

Jon was trying to reconcile the young Thyme with the woman he had only just met. He felt bound to speak up for her. "They were very young. It must have been difficult for her too. They were together for a long time," he said.

"I know. She had her aunt. They were close. She'd had to rely on her a lot with those parents. Her dad left when she was little and her mother had some funny ideas. I thought I could talk Bella round but she's as bitter now as she was then. It doesn't help that Ollie hasn't been back to visit since ... and then, as I said, Thyme turns up as bold as you like."

"How did he feel about the split?"

"He wouldn't discuss it at the time and now we only talk on Skype. It's not the sort of thing you want to air over a computer screen. Bella hardly ever mentions it but I know it's been troubling her a lot. When she heard Thyme was back, it all came out. She said some awful things. I don't know what to do. I thought you might try and put things into perspective for her. She has to forgive Thyme. I don't want her to make herself ill."

"Forgiveness, that's a tricky one."

"She got so worked up the other night I thought she might have a heart attack. It was Marion's idea for me to come and see you. She's as worried as I am."

"Marion Grey?"

"Yes, her sister ... you didn't know they were related?"

"I'm sure someone must have told me," Jon said.

"Sorry, I should have explained at the beginning. It's funny, but you've slotted into the parish so well I'd forgotten you've only been here a couple of months."

"That's nice. I'm glad I've slotted in. I'm happy to call round for a chat with Bella if you think it would help." He reached for his diary and flipped over a couple of pages. "This afternoon's a no-no I'm afraid. It's another busy weekend. It'll have to be tomorrow ... any good?" Ben nodded. "What time?"

"Whatever suits you; Bella doesn't go out unless I take her."

"Shall we say ten thirty?"

"That's fine." Ben stood up and hoisted his trousers into place. "Thanks I'll see you tomorrow, then."

Jon walked over to put an arm round the old man's well-padded shoulders. "Will you tell her I'm coming?" He nodded. "It'll be all right, Ben; try not to worry too much."

"Easier said than done," he said as he shuffled towards the door. "I love her ... always have, always will, whatever funny ideas she gets into her head."

Jon paced about the room after he'd gone. Thyme's problems were becoming clear to him ... a difficult childhood; the death of a favourite aunt; a love affair gone wrong ... he knew about those. Lucy hadn't liked it when he had told her he was leaving the restaurant and going into the church. She had said she didn't want to be a vicar's wife. Her life was corporate entertaining. It was hurtful that she loved money and prestige more than she loved him.

The split had been difficult for both of them but he at least had the certainty of knowing that he was doing the right thing.

Sorting through Thyme's emotional baggage would not be easy, but then, nothing ever was. He was still waiting for her to call. He reckoned she must have been discharged by now. He needed to know why her relationship with Ollie had faltered. His mother had told him what she could. He couldn't ask Daisy. She was at home nursing a bad cold and anyway she didn't seem to know much about the family and then he remembered Nuala was in church. It was a long shot but she might recall something that would help him sort things out.

He walked swiftly over to the door and through the adjoining corridor. He could hear the metallic chink of a bucket being dragged across the flags and detected the evocative scent of freshly cut chrysanthemums. Lent was only days away and then there would be no flowers in church until Easter. It was a bleak time in the church's year and not his favourite but it was also a time for reflection and prayer; a time for taking stock. A time for spring cleaning lives as well as buildings ... an appropriate time for him to help Bella with the dusty corners of hers.

"Were you looking for me, reverend?" Nuala's permed hair was dyed a vibrant orange and although she was small, he reckoned her personality gave her the footprint of an Amazon. He had already learned that he could rely on her to say what she meant and to do what she had promised. She managed the flower budget and arranged the rotas efficiently. He thought she embodied the best of old-fashioned Christianity, a sense of service with strength of mind and steadfast faith. She was the only member of the congregation who addressed him as 'reverend'. He loved the way she said it, rolling her 'r's with relish. "Yes, I was thinking about Easter flowers. How do we go about that here?"

"I'll be putting up the list for Easter lilies in a couple of weeks. We'll have plenty of donations, we always do. Did you want to do something special?"

"I was thinking of an Easter garden."

"Och we do that too," she said. "We usually get the children to help out."

"I'm glad you're so organised," he said. "I'm still feeling my way. Have you heard how Thyme's getting on?"

"That poor wee lass; she's not had a happy life ... aye she's doing well. I called in at the cake shop to ask. She'll be staying with her brother for a few days when she comes out of hospital."

Thyme had told him that. He was annoyed he had not thought of going to the cake shop, himself. "I was thinking of calling in on her again to see how she's doing. I feel sort of responsible with the accident happening outside church."

"I'm sure she'd like that, reverend. Too many people judge," she said.

It was an intriguing remark if a little too enigmatic for his liking. He wished she would enlarge on it but he could not ask what she meant. She might realise he had begun to take a personal interest in Thyme Sykes and he did not want to give himself away; the idea that he was taking a special interest in anyone would give the parish jungle drummers an apoplectic fit. He decided on a nonchalant approach. "I'll pop in next week some time."

"It's not as if she comes to church," Nuala said. "Neither does her brother but it would be a good Christian gesture." She picked up the bucket and tucked the dustpan and brush under her arm. "Well, I'm off now."

"Right," he said. "The flowers look lovely, by the way."

She beamed at him. "Thanks. I do my best."

CHAPTER 13

There had been eight communicants at early morning mass; two up on the previous week. Jon saw it as a positive sign. Sitting in the empty church, he pondered as to how he could encourage a higher attendance. His idea had been to offer a daily service for those who could not be at church at the weekend. He enjoyed starting his day in this way; he reckoned if there were only one other person taking communion with him, then it was worthwhile ... but he would have liked more.

He contemplated the day ahead. He liked a challenge. He doubted Bella would welcome him with open arms but Ben had asked for his help. The situation needed a sensitive approach and careful handling or he could do more harm than good. He was also looking forward to visiting her to find out what else there was to know about Thyme.

He heard footsteps in the vestry, mumbles of conversation. The broom cupboard opened and with it the accompanying clatter of mops and buckets, he had forgotten the spruce-up gang were due; he didn't want to get into a discussion about whose turn it was to polish the brass. He got to his feet. There were calls to be made. Perhaps there would be a message from her waiting for him when he returned.

The cake shop smelled sweet, appetising; full of promise. Gemma had served two customers while Neil waited; one white tin loaf and a box of assorted cakes. She stepped away from the till and tweaked her apron. "What can I get you?"

"Thyme will be home this afternoon. I thought I'd have a welcome home cake ready," he said.

"You must be her brother."
"That's right."
"How is she?"
"Still a bit sore but she's much better, surprised all the doctors with the way she's recovered."
"Can she get about now?"
"They've shown her how to use the crutches and climb the stairs; she practises every day but she won't be running a marathon any time soon."
"They're good up at the hospital. It was such a shock. I was only chatting to her the day before and then ... boom ... just like that," she said thumping her left hand with her right fist.
"Indeed. I think I'll have a chocolate sponge. That one at the front," he said tapping the glass counter to indicate his choice.
"She won't be able to work for a while," Gemma said as she flipped a cake box from flat to 3D.
"No, I'm thinking of taking her away for a few days."
"Where are you going?"
"Cornwall."
"That's nice," she said as she handed over the packaged cake. "I thought you were going to say, Scotland, but that's a bit far with her leg. I don't suppose her son's been down to visit."
"Her son?"
"Yeah ... the one who works with the mountain rescue."
"Thyme doesn't have a son."
"No?" She looked perplexed. "What *am* I like? I must have been thinking of someone else."
"How much?" he said holding up the box.
"Sorry ... I don't know what's the matter with me today ... four pounds fifty. Thanks. Send her my love."

Jon rang the bell and waited. He heard Ben's lumbering footsteps approach the door. "Come in, come in," he said treating Jon to his familiar gap-toothed grin. "She's expecting you."

Bella was sitting on the sofa with Mimi on her knees. It was unusually quiet in the room. She was clutching the remote even though the television was switched off, which he suspected was Ben's doing.

"Fr. Jon's here," he said unnecessarily.

Mimi yapped and Bella shushed her. "I know," she said offering him the same steely glare she had shown to her sister.

"Hello ... how are you Bella?" Jon said.

"Ben thinks I should talk to someone about my *issues,*" she said. "And you pulled the short straw."

He laughed. "It goes with the territory. May I sit down?"

"Sit here," Ben said. He got up from the armchair facing the sofa. "There's something I've forgotten to do." As Bella whispered to Mimi and stroked her back, he winked at Jon and ambled out of the room.

"I understand you're master-minding our raffle," Jon said. "I'm impressed by the amount of support I've had with all the fund-raising."

"We're keen to have that new organ. Look, I'm sorry you've been dragged into this," she said. "I don't mean to be rude but I don't think talking to you is going to help. I only agreed to please Ben."

"Tell me about your son," Jon said. "Ben said he's in New Zealand."

"He's been there for years," she said.

"Do you hear from him much?"

"He doesn't write but we get the odd email ... sometimes he skypes us. I like to see his face on the screen. I like to hear his voice." Suddenly her face crumpled and tears spilled from her eyes. She plucked a tissue from the box next to her and dabbed at her cheeks. "I wasn't going to do this," she said and blew her nose like a trumpet. Mimi whined and jumped to the floor. She padded around Jon's shoes, sniffing the hems of his trousers with studied delicacy before she launched herself back onto Bella's knee. Bella stroked her head in an absent-minded manner.

"I didn't mean to upset you," Jon said. "I expect you miss him."

"Every minute of every day," she said. "He'd still be here if it wasn't for her."

"You mean Thyme."

"Yes, Thyme," she said bitterly. "It was her fault he went. They were engaged to be married. She dumped him. Ollie wouldn't have gone if it hadn't been for her. The poor boy was broken-hearted when they split up. He's never been back, not even for a visit."

"So it was a shock when you heard she had come back."

"More of a horror ... what does she want? She's not welcome round here. She should have stayed away."

"Her brother lives nearby. Her aunt died recently."

"What about her father?"

"I don't know about him."

"He waltzed off to Spain without his wife and children; like father like daughter."

"That's sad but relationships have a habit of breaking down, especially when you're young. People change their minds. We don't know ourselves until we're older. I thought I was going to be a chef until I realised I wanted to go into the ministry. Children leave home, move away whether they have an unhappy love affair or not. I did the same thing myself."

"You didn't go all the way to New Zealand though, did you and now you're back." She glared at him again. "That girl has ruined my life."

"Is your son happy in New Zealand?"

"He seems to be, why?"

"I was thinking I'd be pleased if my son had found a good

job he enjoyed, even if it meant he had to live miles away."

"New Zealand is too far away."

"Daisy has some New Zealanders staying with her."

"I know."

"Can't you go over and see him?" Ben re-appeared and sat down next to Bella on the sofa.

"I don't fly," she said. "It's my blood pressure."

"The doctor said your blood pressure was fine," he said.

"That's not the point," she said rounding on him. "The whole idea of travel makes it go sky high, you know it does. I'm practically house-bound now."

"I don't know your son," Jon said "But if you told him you were so unhappy perhaps he would try and make the trip back home to see you."

"What would be the point of that? He'd only have to go back again," Bella said her eyes flashing in an alarming manner.

Jon could see he was not winning the argument but he wasn't prepared to give up so soon. "Thyme and Ollie broke up a long time ago; it was their relationship that failed, not yours with your son. Perhaps now is the time to let the unhappiness go, to allow yourself to forgive and forget."

"Why does everyone say that? I don't want to forget and I certainly won't ever forgive her. She's evil, that's what she is."

"Bella," Ben protested. "That's a bit strong. I quite liked the girl. I know you don't agree with me but Ollie could be a bit selfish at times. We don't know how good their relationship was or how good it would have been after a few more years together. You never allowed her to explain. You tore up all her letters. A clean break was probably best."

The veins in Bella's neck stood out as she tried to control her rage. She rose to her feet. "I know my son and I know what *she* did. All this talk is giving me a headache. I need to lie down," she said and taking Mimi in her arms she left the room.

Ben stared after her, his shoulders hunched. “See,” he said. “That’s what she’s like. Perhaps it wasn’t such a good idea after all.”

“Forgiveness is hard,” Jon said. “You have to let go of the feelings and thoughts that have become a part of you over the years. Resentment takes hold and letting go of it is like letting go of a part of yourself ... and then you have to find something else to fill that gap.”

“Like what?”

“Hopefully reconciliation and peace of mind but it doesn’t always work that way.”

“I’d like Bella to find some peace. She used to be such a lovely bubbly person. I wish you’d known her then.”

“I’m sure the old Bella is still in there. We just need to coax her out again, persuade her it’s possible to let go of the grudge she’s been bearing all these years, make her see that Thyme isn’t the bad person she thinks she is.”

“How do we do that?”

“I don’t know yet, but I’m going to give it some serious thought and prayer.”

Ben sighed. “I’m beginning to wish I hadn’t tried to help. It’s only made matters worse.”

“Sometimes things have to get worse before they get better. I’m glad you came to see me. If we keep talking we will eventually see our way through. Not talking is the way things fall apart and we don’t want that.”

“I doubt she’ll ever come round.”

“We have to think positive. I believe she will. Keep trying, Ben. It would be good if you could get Ollie on side.”

“I don’t know about that.”

“We’ll talk again when she’s had time to think it over. Are you going to the Committee meeting tonight? I can’t make it I’m afraid.”

He shrugged. “Probably not ... it depends on Bella.”

"I'll pop in after the weekend, see how things are."

"Thanks, vicar. I'm sorry to have wasted your time."

"It wasn't a waste of time. I'm here to help in whatever way I can. I'm not giving up yet."

CHAPTER 14

Daisy had taken Diana's words to heart. It was with her sensible head on that she rang Vi a couple of days later. "I wondered if you could do me a favour," she said.

"You don't sound too good."

"This cold is dragging on. My voice is going. I don't feel up to hosting the committee meeting. Could you do it?"

Vi Tracey's family had lived in Upfordham for ever. There weren't many of them left now, just Vi and her cousin, Devlin. He lived the life of a hermit down by the coast in a ramshackle smuggler's cottage. She didn't see him very often. The church filled the gaps in her life. Her Victorian cottage had no front garden, just a couple of window boxes full of bulbs biding their time and long arms of Wisteria clinging to the front wall. The orchards at the back had been transformed into a housing estate; trampolines, not trees, crested the sky-line, but it had a through lounge, spacious enough to seat everyone. "You mean have the committee meeting here," she said.

"If you don't mind ..."

"No, I'm happy to step into the breach, so to speak. Have you told the others?"

"Not yet, could you give them a ring?"

"Don't worry ... I'll sort it all out."

The fund-raising committee was now assembled in her lounge while she was in the kitchen counting cups onto a tray with Joan Drabble. "I'm glad you decided to join us after all," she said.

"I thought I might as well. There weren't many volunteers and Daisy would have ended up doing most of it herself. How is she?"

"Over the worst," Vi said. "Her chest's been bad but she'll be at the auction tomorrow."

"Oh yes. Diana Driver's painting. I wonder how much it will go for."

"Daisy said they were hoping for at least a thousand pounds."

"Wouldn't that be great?"

"I've been over to Tom Briggs' place you know," Vi said.

"Have you?"

"I took my grandmother's clock down there when Dev's old fridge conked out. He said he didn't want another one, but it gets so hot in his little place in the summer; I didn't want him to end up with food poisoning. I told him I'd buy him a new one with a freezer compartment and I'd fill it up with pies."

"I bet he liked that."

"He loves his food. I suppose I shouldn't encourage him but what other pleasures does he have?"

"Erm ... cigarettes?"

"Yes, there is that."

"Has he tried to stop?"

Vi shook her head. "He'll never do it now. Do you know where Ben is?"

"No ... perhaps he didn't want to leave Bella on her own ... she hasn't been herself lately."

"Marion said she's been a bit funny since the accident."

"I'd love to know what Thyme's doing back here."

"The vicar's been round."

"What ... round to see Bella?"

"Yes."

"How do you know?"

"Marion told me earlier."

"Well let's hope he made her see sense." Vi hoisted the steaming kettle over to the table and filled up the pot. "There, that should do it. Bring the biscuits would you, I'll carry the tray ..." she said backing out into the hall "... it sounds as if Owen's on his soap box about the raffle again."

"Marion will be going mad in there," Joan whispered back as they approached the open door. "She's already sorted it all out with Bella."

"Deep breath and in we go." Vi elbowed the door wide, cups and saucers chinking on the tray.

Owen was resting an elbow on the mantelpiece of the ultra-tidy room, his foot on the hearthstone. Marion was sitting next to Rachel on the sofa, reclining against a fluffy blanket which hid the warn moquette and a cigarette burn caused by Devlin months before. Her expression was tightly controlled. "I'll bear that in mind," she said.

"And we need a few decent items, not boxes and boxes of biscuits and cheap chocolates," he went on. "No-one wants to take home cheap chocolates. Don't you agree, Rachel?"

"Don't involve me," Rachel said. "I shouldn't be here. I'm not on the committee. I'm just serving teas at the fair."

The tray landed on the coffee table with a clatter. "I'll be mother, shall I?" Vi said.

"Milk and two," Owen said. "Have we discussed everything now?"

"I should think so," Rachel said.

"I've made notes for Daisy," Vi said. "Will you tell Ben what we've decided?"

"Certainly and I'll ask Angela about the cards."

"Thanks. Let Daisy know what she says and if she wants a table to herself. She likes to make a plan of the hall in advance or we end up juggling tables on the day and people get annoyed if they have to move."

"I can help with that."

"Have a word with Daisy."

He opened his file and clicked the top of his pen with a

flourish. “Check on raffle ...” he said as he wrote. Marion frowned at Vi who hid her smile in her teacup. “Ask Angela about cards. Tell Ben ... and check with Daisy about tables,” he added. “Is that it?”

Rachel rattled her cup on the saucer. “I don’t know where we’d be without you, Owen,” she said. “Would you like to serve teas, too?”

“I don’t think so,” he said. “I’ll be too busy supervising.”

Neil propped his shoulder against the door-frame and watched his wife tapping away on the keyboard. “Amy’s in bed,” he said.

“Thanks. If I don’t get this finished tonight, I’ll be in trouble.”

“I’m worried about Thyme.”

She swivelled away from the desk to face him, pushing her glasses to the top of her head. “She seems much more mobile to me,” she said.

“Not physically. I’m worried about her mental state. I’ve told her about Cornwall.”

“What did she say?”

“She’s thinking about it.”

“I haven’t had a chance to spend much time with her over the past few days. I’ll make up for it over the weekend ... we can have a heart to heart if she wants. We still haven’t discussed the accident properly. I never seem to have time for anything these days.”

“I don’t think she wants to talk about it,” Neil said.

“She needs to talk; she could end up with post traumatic stress if she doesn’t.”

“Since when have you been a psychiatrist?”

“Bottling things up is never good ... you were the one who said there was something she wasn’t telling us.”

“I know but I don’t want to upset her.”

"I won't do that."

"I suppose it's worth a try. She's certainly not telling me anything but wait until the weekend. I said I'd go round to the flat tomorrow. Sorting through Aunt Lal's belongings might unsettle her."

"I'm known for my tact," Chantal said, "Unlike you. If you keep asking her what's wrong you'll just freak her out. We all get down from time to time and she's just lost her favourite aunt. I'd say that was reason enough to be depressed."

"I bow to your superior knowledge, o wise one," Neil said bowing in a deferential fashion. "You could be right."

"When am I not?"

Thyme sat in the newly re-furbished kitchen the following morning and toyed with a croissant. "So, have you had time to think about Cornwall?" Neil asked.

"Not really. I don't know."

"A change of scene might do you good."

"Maybe we could go in the summer. I don't want to be a nuisance. I might go away with Jill to give you a break."

"Are you sure you're up to it?"

"We'll be in the car ... I won't have to walk far."

"Well, if that's what you want. I'm off now," he said.

"Sorry I can't help," she said trying to lift her metal-braced leg in his direction. "Don't throw anything away until I've seen it."

"I won't. Did Chantal give you that box? It's everything I emptied from her dressing table."

"I thought I'd take a look while you're out."

"Ok. What shall I do with her clothes?"

"Go through the pockets, check for brooches or money and then bag them. We'll take them to Oxfam after I'm sure there's nothing we can use, that was her favourite charity. They should make a fair amount of money. She had some good stuff."

"Will they take the shoes, too?"

"They'll take anything within reason."

"I need to get started. We haven't got long left. I'm glad we had the furniture collected last week."

"It's just the built-in wardrobe and the kitchen cupboards now ..."

"And all the books," he said.

"Yes ... the books ... we need to weed out the good ones."

"What about the law books?"

"We might be able to sell some of them on ebay. Hard up students might be grateful for a cheap copy."

"I'll collect some boxes from the supermarket and move as many as I can. I'll be back to get your lunch."

"Don't bother about that. I haven't got much of an appetite."

"I'd noticed. I'm worried about you."

"There's no need, little brother. I've still got some cake left to nibble on. I'll be fine until tonight."

"That's not what I meant."

"I know ... look, Neil, I'll sort myself out, ok?"

She waited until she heard his car crunch off the drive and then taking a black bin bag from the kitchen drawer she hobbled over to the cardboard box he had left on the dining room table. She stripped back the sticky tape holding it together and lifted out two carrier bags filled with what looked like costume jewellery and some small boxes containing what she hoped were more interesting items.

There were several hairbrushes and half-used bottles of perfume, which she threw straight in the bin bag. She dumped the dimpled tubes of make-up, hand cream and body lotion and then sat down to investigate the other items.

She recalled Aunt Lal wearing the long strings of beads; green glass, nuggets of amber, pellets of acrylic the colour of the Mediterranean, plus numerous multi-coloured, multi-strand necklaces. She put the jet beads to one side and the long string of pearls that she remembered her aunt saying had belonged to her mother and dropped the rest of the finery back into the bag ready for the girls to look through when they came home from school. She had decided that if nothing appealed, the whole lot could go to Oxfam with the clothes.

There were no earrings. Aunt Lal had never had her ears pierced. She debated whether she wanted the gold bangle she had found wrapped in a velvet bag. She slipped it on her wrist while she made up her mind and then examined the rings. One antique garnet set with pearls; the gold and onyx signet ring that Aunt Lal had worn every day of her life; she would keep that and a diamond ring ... the diamond ring ... *her* diamond ring.

It flashed and sparkled at her in a beguiling fashion. It was tempting; so tempting she could not resist. She slid it over the knuckle on the third finger of her left hand remembering the excitement she had felt when Ollie had given it to her and the promises he had made. She felt regret for the life she thought they had mapped out together and sad it had ended badly.

She moved her hand this way and that as she had done then. She watched the fire come and go as the light caught the stone, recalling her feelings of emptiness when she had dragged it from her finger and handed it over to Aunt Lal all those years ago. Ollie had said she could keep it but just looking at it had made her weep. Aunt Lal said she would make it disappear and she hadn't cared what had happened to it after that. From then on she had blanked it from her mind. It represented one big lie after another, not the love commitment and hope it should have done. She had never asked about it. She presumed it had been sold.

She tugged it roughly from her finger and re-placed it in its box, snapping the catch firmly. She felt her throat tighten. She tried to swallow down the tears and when that failed she took a deep breath in an effort to will the misery away but raw grief had taken hold. Her mouth began to tremble; her whole face went into melt-down and then she sobbed and sobbed as if her heart would break.

CHAPTER 15

The doors to the sale room were wide open when Daisy arrived. She could hear Tom's voice talking up a Victorian writing slope "... it's lovely polished oak; you wouldn't get that patina on plastic ... I can start the bidding at sixty pounds ... sixty pounds with me; where's seventy? Come on ladies ... think of all the love letters you could write on this ... think of all the ones already written ... sixty-five then ... it's well worth the money ..."

She paid for a catalogue and went through to the body of the hall as he got a bite at sixty-five. After weaving her way through the crowd she found Diana sitting on a balloon-backed chair surrounded by a bevy of bidders; the eyes of the hall were on Tom who was wearing one of his trademark waistcoats. She edged her way through. "I hope they're more forthcoming with their money when it comes to oil paintings," she murmured, her voice still husky from her cold. "Let's go and stand at the back." Diana extricated herself from the crowd to follow her to an open space she had found by a mahogany display cupboard loaded with china. "It's busy in here ... when's it coming up?"

"It shouldn't be long now," Diana said. "How's the cold?"

"Not too bad ... I hope it does better than the writing slope."

"Tom had to work hard for that one."

"Fingers crossed they're into art."

"That's the problem with auctions. You can never tell what will happen."

"Where have they put it?"

"It's on the wall by the window."

Daisy followed Diana's gaze. The dogs formed part of a

wall of pictures, sandwiched between a pastel of a young man in full army uniform and an oil painting of a Victorian patriarch sporting fine mutton-chop whiskers. “Oh yes ... ah, they’re so sweet.”

“Fifteen hundred pounds sweet, do you think?”

Daisy covered her mouth with her scarf and emitted a barking cough. “Sorry ... could be ... it’s a much more attractive proposition than any of the others up there ... or someone’s unmade bed and that made a fortune.”

“Do you think we’re getting old and set in our ways?” Diana said.

“Perish the thought,” Daisy said flipping back frothy curls and showing off slate grey nails. “You’re still looking pretty good and so am I. We both like to keep up to date with things. We know what we like, that’s all.”

“An eye for beauty,” Diana said.

“He’s quite an eyeful,” Daisy said winking in Tom’s direction.

“Daisy really ... I can see you’re feeling better. He’s half our age.”

“So? I’m sure I could teach him a trick or two.”

“I don’t want to think about that,” Diana said. Daisy laughed which ended in another coughing fit. “Are you sure you’re ok?”

“I’m fine. It’s very dry in here. A change of air always makes me cough. Anyway I hate being cooped up. I’m glad to be out.”

“Do you need a drink? I’ve got a bottle of water in my bag.”

“I bought some cough sweets on my way over.” She rummaged in her pocket to retrieve the sweets, tore open the tube and popped one into her mouth. “That’s better ... I’m fine now.”

“Here we go,” Diana said. “This is it.”

Neil returned to the house with the car full of bin bags and two boxes of books. He found Thyme reclining on the sofa. "How did you get on," she said.

"Ok ... I've checked and bagged everything as ordered. Do you want me to bring the bags in here?"

"No ... I don't have the energy to tackle all that this afternoon."

"No problem. I'll leave them in the garage for now." He felt in the pocket of his jeans. "I found this on the lapel of her winter coat," he said, dropping a tarnished brooch into her palm. "It looks like a seahorse."

She felt the tears welling up again. "It's a kelpie," she said. "Aunt Lal had a thing about kelpies."

"I've never heard of them."

"They're Scottish and a bit dark ... mythical water spirits that turn into horses on land. There's a big sculpture up in Falkirk and a smaller version at Edinburgh airport."

"It looks like silver. It should polish up. The girls will be back soon. Show it to Amy. She's mad about horses; I'm sure she'd like to hear all about the kelpies. Did you find anything you wanted to keep?"

"A few things ... the girls can look through the rest and Chantal if she wants. If they don't see anything they like it can all go to Oxfam with the clothes."

"We're nearly there now. I checked the kitchen cupboards. There wasn't much."

"She didn't like cooking. We ate out unless I cooked."

"I reckon another day should do it."

"Good."

"Do you want me to drive you over for one last look?"

She shook her head. "I've said my goodbyes."

"That was disappointing," Diana said.

"Will you try again next month?"

"I don't know. I was sure it would sell but not even to reach the reserve ..."

"What you need is a stiff gin."

"I'll settle for lunch at Sue's Place."

"Did you come in the car?"

"Yes ... did you."

"I cycled round; I'll meet you there but I won't be able to hang about. I promised to be at Maggie's when the prospective purchasers come round. The estate agent's double booked himself."

"Was it David Reedman?"

"No, it was one of the Linchester ones," she said and then balanced the bike between her knees so that she could enjoy another good cough before she set off. "See you in a minute," she called as she gave a cheery wave and pedalled away.

Diana walked into the car park to find Jon just about to leave his motorbike. He hurried towards her, helmet tucked under his arm like nearly headless Nick. He bent down to kiss her cheek. "Have I missed it?" he said. "I couldn't get away any earlier ... sorry."

"You will never believe what happened."

"It made millions," he said with a grin.

"It didn't even reach the reserve."

"That's a shame."

"I'm so sorry. I was positive it would sell."

"Don't worry about it..."

"I'm really annoyed. It was all going into your fund."

"Perhaps you were meant to keep it."

"I'd rather you had the cash. I'll speak to Tom ... see what he advises. He'll be disappointed. He was sure it would make the money, too."

"I saw Daisy cycling out. I didn't know she was coming; is she better now?"

"She seems fine, still coughing a bit but on good form.

We're off to Sue's Place to cry into our soup. Will you join us?"

"I've got too many loose ends to tie up before my long weekend."

"Oh yes ... I'd forgotten you were going away."

"It's only four days but I need it. I'm going as far as I can ... out of reach of mobile phones and then perhaps I can switch off and get on with the writing."

"Why don't you go up to Cath's? The reception over there is awful."

"It's hardly quiet though. Jack will want me to play cricket and the others will be tearing all over the house ... with Easter coming up I need to re-charge my batteries as well as the writing."

"Dad used to say everyone thinks Christmas is the busiest time for a priest but it's not, Easter is much busier. Have you seen Thyme? She must be out of hospital now."

"No ... look, I'll give you a bell before I go. I'm off to have a chat with Tom. Shall I mention the picture?"

"No, leave it. I'll speak to him later."

"Ok. Enjoy your lunch."

Tom was still on the rostrum when Jon moved inside. He found a seat near the back and didn't have to wait long before the gavel was passed to a colleague. He stood up and caught his eye almost at once. "Tom, it's good to see you."

"You look pretty impressive," Tom said as he gripped his hand.

"You like the leathers?"

"You haven't still got the Norton have you?"

"Of course ... there's no other way to travel. I see you haven't lost your bad taste," he said patting the vibrant waistcoat.

"I have a certain reputation to maintain," Tom said.

"Do you have time to see me now?"

"I can give you half an hour ... shame about the painting."

"I wasn't going to mention it."

"I don't know what happened. It should have made at least fifteen hundred. Your mum must be disappointed."

"She said she'd call you."

"Ok ... come into the boardroom," he said ushering Jon into a large-ish room decorated in Union Jack stripes. Jon winced and shielded his eyes with his hands. Tom laughed. "Don't you like my interior decor?"

"It's very you."

"Take a seat. What can I do for you?"

"Mum told me about your mother. I'm so sorry."

"It's not much fun," he said, the bantering tone, gone.

"I know, mate. How is she?"

"Not good. They don't seem to know how much worse it will get. Apparently every case is different but it's bad enough already; she's not my mum now. She still looks like Mum; she's got Mum's voice but she doesn't talk like her or react in the same way. My mum was always confident, out-going, the life and soul ... well, you remember."

"I do and you'll still have those memories. It's just a question of hanging on in there; taking one day at a time. How are the children?"

"How you would expect ... frightened one minute; impatient the next. We keep thinking that we'll get up one morning and she won't be there. It's like living on a knife edge."

"What can I do? I'm happy to come and see her. Would that help?"

"She might not remember you but I'd appreciate it; I don't go out in the evenings if I can help it. The kids would sit with her but I don't think it's fair to expect them to put their lives on hold too."

"No ... it must be hard. Somehow you expect your parents to go on for ever."

“It won’t be the same without her.”

“You’re doing everything you can, mate. No-one could ask for more. I’m away for the next few days but I’ll be round as soon as I get back, that’s a promise.”

CHAPTER 16

The silver brooch nestled in the palm of Amy's hand, gleaming like a fallen star. "Would you like to keep it?"

She dragged her eyes away. "Yes pleeeese. I love it."

"Well, it's yours. You don't want any of these beads?"

She leaned forward to scratch her back and then she shook her head. "No, thanks ... I'll just take the kelpie. What *is* a kelpie, Thyme?"

"It's an imaginary creature, a shape-shifting water spirit that can turn into a horse when it leaves the water and steps onto land. They were supposed to haunt the lakes and rivers of Scotland, snatching passers-by who were silly enough to come too close," she said suddenly encircling Amy in her arms and hugging her tight. She squealed but did not try to escape. "There's a big sculpture of them up in Scotland. When my leg's better, I'll take you to see it."

"I've never been to Scotland."

Thyme relaxed her arms and started to pack up the rest of the jewellery. "We'll ask your mum and dad if we can go in the Easter holidays. What's the matter with your back?" she said as Amy wriggled in her seat moving her shoulders sideways and then up and down against the back of the chair like a cow on a fence post.

"Dunno. It's itchy."

"Perhaps you've got fleas."

"Dogs and cats get fleas, not children," she said prosaically.

"Are you quite sure?" Thyme teased. Amy giggled.

"Bath time," Neil said as he appeared at the dining room door.

"Look what Thyme's given me," she said skipping across to show him her treasure.

"Hmm ... it's lovely."

"We're going to Scotland to see the sculpture," she said.

"Are you now, who said?"

"Thyme did. We are, aren't we?" she said swivelling round on one leg to seek confirmation."

Thyme smiled. "I promised," she said.

"Yippee," Amy said and ran off upstairs.

"I hope she hasn't been annoying you."

"Not at all, we've been talking about Aunt Lal ... and kelpies of course. I enjoy her company. She loves animals."

"Yes. We haven't got round to organising those riding lessons yet. I can remember you going riding."

"I might take it up again. We could go together."

"So you can break the other leg," he said.

"I won't fall off. I've never been thrown."

"There's a first time for everything. Alice is waiting for you to come and see the film."

"I'll put these away and hobble through, start without me."

"You'll soon pick up the story; most of these teenage musicals are the same; boy hates girl, girl hates boy; girl hates girl even more, they all love each other at the end."

She laughed. "I get the picture. Which one is it?"

"She's chosen 'Pitch Perfect'; it's one of the better ones. I think it's quite amusing."

"You're an expert?" she said.

"I live in a house full of women what did you expect?"

"Shock, horror ... you're not turning into a metro sexual are you?"

"I could be something a lot worse," he said. "Hurry up or you'll miss most of it."

Thyme was happy to watch the film but she was too tired to stay awake. The third time Neil nudged her arm she decided it was time to leave. She smothered another yawn. "Does anyone mind if I go to bed?"

"It's only nine o'clock," Alice said. She was stretched out on her stomach, chin propped up on her elbows, eyes glued to the screen. "You haven't seen the best bit yet."

"It's a DVD," Neil said. "She can watch it any time." He scrutinised his sister's face. She looked thinner than ever, her skin almost transparent. "Is everything all right?"

"Apart from a broken leg you mean?" she said with a spark.

Chantal un-tucked her legs from the sofa cushions and pushed her glasses up into her hair. "We don't mind," she said. "You must be tired."

"I am. See you in the morning."

"It's time you went to bed, too, Alice," Neil said. "It's school tomorrow."

"Come on, Dad. This will be finished soon."

"You've got half an hour. If it's not finished then, it's going off." She pulled a face at him but resisted the urge to make further comment.

Chantal eased herself up from the sofa. "I'm going to make a drink. Do you want one, Neil?"

He followed her in to the kitchen. "Do you think she's ok?"

"She's fine, just being a teenager."

"I meant my sister."

"Oh, well, she's bound to be tired. Her body's been knocked about," she said.

"She doesn't want to go to Cornwall."

"You can't make her."

"I thought it would cheer her up ... change of scene, sea air. We went there a lot as kids. I couldn't take her now anyway. I've just found out I've got an article to finish by Friday."

"It's just as well she doesn't want to go."

"She wants us to take Amy up to Scotland to see the kelpies.

"That's good. It shows she's thinking positive."

“She hasn’t had many visitors. I thought someone from the church might have popped in. Do you think I should ring the vicar? He visited her in hospital. She might talk to him. She liked his dad ... we both liked him.”

“The famous rector you’re always going on about.”

“Yes, look, I know something’s bothering her but she obviously doesn’t want to say.”

“I tried talking to her last night. She said there was nothing wrong. Perhaps you’re imagining it. If she’s making plans that can only be good. How did you get on at the flat?”

“I cleared all the clothes and started on the books. She hasn’t been through them yet. They’re still in the garage.”

“She might not be ready to deal with them at the moment. Don’t hassle her about it.”

“It could just be grief. She seemed back to normal when she was talking with Amy.”

“Perhaps you *should* speak to the vicar. He’ll be used to dealing with bereavement. He’ll know what to say and it might stop you worrying.”

“She won’t thank me for interfering,” he said.

“She doesn’t need to find out. Ask the vicar not to involve you. He must have dealt with similar situations a million times before, you know, helping concerned families.”

His expression lifted. “You could have something there. I hadn’t thought of that. I might give him a call now ... see what he says.”

“It’s a bit late to phone now.”

“I can leave a message.”

“Do it tomorrow.”

The door opened slowly to reveal a tousled Amy, her cheeks flushed. “Mum ...”

“What is it babs? I thought you were asleep.”

“I’ve got a headache.”

“Oh dear, let’s have a look at you.” She felt Amy’s

forehead. “I was hoping this wouldn’t happen,” she said peering at her daughter’s neck and then at her back which revealed a crop of small blister-like spots. “Come and see this, Neil.”

“What is it?”

“What’s the matter with me?” Amy said as she struggled to escape her mother’s restraining arm.

“I think you might have chicken pox,” Chantal said. She turned Amy round and lifted the back of her pyjamas to show him the evidence. “Three children in your year have already come down with it.”

“I thought she had it when she was a baby.”

Chantal sat down, balancing Amy on her knees. “That was Alice. Amy didn’t catch it. I was still breast-feeding. She must have got some immunity from me.”

“That’ll be at least a week off school,” he said.

Amy’s face lit up. “Yippee.”

“It’s a good job I’m here,” he added.

“Has Thyme had chicken pox?” Chantal said.

“She had it the same time as me. We were both covered in spots; I can remember counting them every night when mum smothered us in calamine lotion.”

“I don’t want spots,” Amy said. “Everyone will laugh at me.”

Chantal stroked her hair. “No-one will see them, babs. By the time you go back to school all the scabs will be gone.”

“I don’t want scabs either.”

“I’m afraid you can’t avoid them but you must try not to scratch too much or they might leave scars.”

Amy’s face crumpled and her eyes filled with tears. “I don’t like scars.”

“Thyme doesn’t have scars and she had even more spots than me,” Neil said. “Ask her tomorrow.”

“I wasn’t thinking about Thyme catching chicken pox,”

Chantal said. "She might develop shingles."

"Do you think she should go home?"

She nodded. "We can't risk it. She hasn't recovered from the accident yet and shingles can be quite nasty."

"What's shingles?" Amy said.

"It's a virus you can catch if you've had chicken pox," Neil said. "I hope she'll be ok on her own."

"Of course she will. You can check on her every day. She'll probably be more relaxed at home anyway. She'll get more rest."

Amy sniffed. "Can I have some Calpol Mum? My head really hurts."

Chantal edged her gently off her knees and took her by the hand. "We'll sort out the Calpol and then I'll come up to bed with you and tuck you in."

CHAPTER 17

"Are you coming to the butcher's?" Ben asked his wife the next morning as he gave her an encouraging smile.

"I'm not talking to you," she said.

"What have I done now?"

"You know what you've done."

"I don't."

"Oh yes you do."

"Panto season's over, love. You're not still cross because I asked Fr. Jon to come and see you, are you?"

"You knew I didn't want to talk about it."

"Well I'd had enough of not talking about it," he said. "I've spent years tiptoeing around you and I've said nothing. It's time you let it go and it's time you stopped blaming Thyme Sykes for everything that's wrong in your life. You need to move on. I'm going now. If you want to come with me you'd better get your coat." He turned tail, leaving a startled Bella to stare after him open-mouthed as he closed the door firmly behind him.

She cuddled Mimi to her. "How could he be so mean?" she asked the dog. "He doesn't understand how I feel. I'll never stop blaming Thyme. It *was* all her fault." She sighed loudly and heaved herself off the sofa dropping the little dog into her basket. "You stay here. I'll bring you a nice piece of chicken."

Ben jumped away from the door and hurried into the kitchen. He took up the pen with which he had been writing a list and pretended to be adding a last-minute item when she sidled up to him. "I'm coming with you," she said.

"Coat," he said tersely. "And hurry up. I don't want to hang around I'm due at the Bandy at half one."

"There's no need to take that tone with me," she said huffily. "And don't think I've changed my mind about Thyme. "I'll never let it go. She's ruined my life and nothing's going to change that ... *ever*."

The following morning Neil made his call to the vicarage and then went in search of his wife. "He's away for a few days," he said. "I left a message on the answer phone."

"What did you say?"

"I asked him to call on her at home."

"Did you ask him to keep you out of it?"

"Yes. I hope she won't be too suspicious when he turns up unannounced."

"She won't. It's what vicar's do, visit the sick. Give Alice a shout, would you, I want to check my messages before we go."

"Mum's ready," he called up the stairs. Moments later Alice emerged from her room with her tie knotted in such a way that one end was ridiculously shorter than the other and with her skirt, way above her knees. "You know what she's going to say to you," he said.

She picked up her school bag and gave him a dark look. "Everyone else does it."

He decided this was one fight too many. "Don't say I didn't warn you. Go and say goodbye to Thyme. I'm taking her home this morning."

Chantal breezed back in and treated him to an airy kiss. "Is she ready?"

"She's just saying goodbye to Thyme."

"Ah here she is, bye darling."

"See you both, later."

Chantal contemplated her daughter's skirt. "You'll have to unroll that before we get there," she said. "And do something with your tie." Alice pulled a face behind her back. "Yessir," she said with an exaggerated salute.

"I know everyone else does it, but we're having a purge on school uniform this week and you don't need a detention."

Neil grinned as he shut the door behind them and ran up the stairs to check on Amy. He found her plugged into her earphones. She tugged one out when she saw him. "You're awake," he said. "How are you feeling?"

"Ok ... still a bit itchy but my headache's gone."

"I'm going out in a minute. I didn't want you to wake up and find you were alone in the house."

"Has Mum gone?"

"Yes she took Alice with her this morning. Are you going to stay in bed a bit longer?"

She nodded. "I don't want my breakfast yet."

"I'll make you some eggy bread when I've dropped Thyme off at home."

"Can I say goodbye to her?"

"You can wave at her from the landing," he said.

She hopped out of bed and padded behind him, stretching along the banister like a sloth.

Thyme caught the movement from above as she stood in the hall waiting for him. "Hi Amy ... I'm sorry you're poorly. I hope you feel better soon," she said.

"Thanks. You can text me if you like."

She smiled up at her. "I will, but only if you text me first."

"Back to bed," Neil said and waited until she had bounced off to her room before he took the stairs two at a time.

"You are lucky, Neil, having children, I mean," Thyme said.

"It's not too late for you."

"I don't know if you'd noticed but I haven't got a partner."

"It's not too late for that either." He helped her down the step and then pushed open the front passenger door of his car. "I'll move this seat for you," he said as he slid it back as far as it would go. "Try that."

She lowered herself, back first onto the seat and then swung her leg across under the dashboard. "There's plenty of room," she said. He shut the door and walked round to the driving seat. "Thanks for having me," she added. "These last few days with you have really helped. I feel more human now."

"Good," he said. He thought she seemed a lot more cheerful and wished he had not been so quick to involve the vicar. Perhaps Chantal was right and all that was wrong with her was a natural sadness at the passing of their aunt. "Are you sure you'll be able to manage on your own?"

"Stop worrying. I've got everything I need downstairs. I've been practising climbing the stairs so I can get up there if I really need to. It's easy so long as I take my time."

"One or other of us will be at home now Amy's ill. Just ring if you need anything."

"I will."

"Have you got enough to eat?"

"I'm sure I have, the freezer's full; stop fussing."

"Give me a bell if you need more shopping."

"For heaven's sake, Neil, I'm not ten years old. I'll manage. Jill said she'd call in later."

He parked as near to the front door as he could. "Ok but if you can't manage just let us know."

She undid her seatbelt and reached for the door catch. "Let me out of here and get back to Amy, she needs you more than I do."

"Have you got the key?"

"Here," she said waving her keys at him.

He took the case and carried it inside, waiting for her to catch up. "Where do you want this?"

"Put it on the kitchen table. I can unpack it there."

"Can I get you a drink or something before I go?"

"No. Off you go *now*," she said shooing him away as if he were a troublesome goose.

“Where are you going to sleep?”

She sighed. “In my bed of course ... I’ll only have to come down and go up again, once a day ... I’ve told you ... I’ll manage.”

“I’ll call you later.” She watched him walk down the path and then closed the door, leaning against it to drink in the silence. It was a blessing and a curse but she needed time to think.

Jon was having trouble casting off from parish matters. “I’m never going to get away at this rate,” he said, exasperated with Daisy’s last minute tick list.

“Just one more thing,” she said Columbo style. “Who are we going to ask to draw the raffle?”

“What are the options?”

“The committee couldn’t decide between the youngest choir member, the oldest parishioner and Owen Reedman.”

“Go for the choir ... is that it?”

“Yes,” she said bundling up her files and dumping them in the leather satchel she always carried on her bike. “I don’t want to delay you; I’m off to see your mum next. We’re trying to organise the book launch.”

“You do realise it’s not finished yet,” he said.

“I know but we have to get give people notice, allow them time to arrange accommodation and all that.”

“It’s a good job I’ve got this long weekend or I might not meet the deadline.”

“You’ll do it,” she said. “We’re giving you until May. That’s plenty of time,” she added with a confident smile.

He smiled back. “You almost make me think I will. You won’t be able to contact me while I’m away. I’m going back to basics.” He picked up the rucksack that had been sitting next to his leather-clad legs. “See?” he said, the chains on his boots jangling as he got to his feet “... travelling light. I’ll be out of reach of the mobile network. Owen knows what to do if there's an emergency."

"I've got all the telephone numbers," she said. "We had to manage without a priest for nearly a year, so I'm sure we can survive a weekend without you."

He picked up the helmet, zipped up his jacket and clicked his heels. "See you on Wednesday." He hoped she wasn't going to follow him out. He planned to call on Thyme before he left for the wilds of Scotland and he didn't want to have to face a barrage of questions on his return. He hadn't been summoned by a phone call from her, but he reckoned her brother's message was sufficient justification if challenged. It had always been his intention to visit her before he went away, phone call or no phone call, but her brother's intervention had validated his decision.

His heart pounded as he drew near the house. The bike spluttered to a halt. He dismounted and wheeled it round to the side, flicking the kick stand with his boot, waiting as it settled into a slight list to the left before he removed his helmet, balanced it on the seat and walked brazenly up to the front door. He rang the bell. As the seconds ticked by his excitement and anticipation slipped away; could he have misunderstood? Perhaps she had changed her mind; she must still be at her brother's house. He was just about to give up and go when the door opened.

His heart started pounding again. "I hope you don't mind me coming round to see you," he began breathlessly. "I'm going away for a few days. I thought I'd check on you before I left."

She stared at him and he thought for a moment that she was going to shut the door in his face. "I'd been wondering when you would turn up," she said. "Come in."

"How are you?"

"Oh ... as well as can be expected."

"I guess you're still a bit bruised."

"Not really. I'm stiff more than anything; it's awkward getting about but I can manage most things."

"That's excellent."

"I have trouble if I drop something; it's tricky getting dressed but on the whole I feel good."

"I'm surprised you're home so soon. I thought you'd be at your brother's for a while."

"One of his daughter's has chicken pox."

"They didn't want you to catch it."

"I've had chicken pox. They were worried about shingles."

"Oh right. I can go away with a clear conscience, then, if you're ok," he said.

"Where are you going?"

"Scotland."

"Lucky you," she said. "I love Scotland."

"Come with me," he said. The words were out of his mouth before he realised their significance. "Sorry, I was only joking. Of course you don't want to come with me." Silence stretched between them like a cat in the sun until he could bear it no longer. "I didn't expect you to take me seriously. I'm really going because I need to finish my book. Did you know I was writing a book? It's a recipe book," he babbled on. "I'm hoping to raise a lot of money for the organ fund." He couldn't see her face; she was staring at the floor and then she raised her eyes to his.

"I'd like to very much," she said, "But not on the back of your motorbike." She smiled and he had the impression that her face was a flower opening for the first time. "Is that rather cheeky of me?"

Surely he had misunderstood. He felt out of his depth. "You'd like to come to Scotland with me?"

"You did ask."

"I know."

“Did you want me to?”

“Yes but ...”

“You don’t sound very sure.”

“I am.” He was and yet he felt like a teenager contemplating a weekend of illicit passion. Excited but scared of being found out.

“Well, my bag’s in the kitchen. I haven’t had time to unpack it yet. We can leave straight away.”

“You’re ready to leave ... you mean, right now?”

She was laughing. “Yes, right now. Life’s too short to pussyfoot around. You’re going to Scotland and I want to hitch a lift. We’ll take my car if you’re worried about getting noticed in yours. No-one will give us a second glance. I hardly ever use it. You can lock your bike in the garage.”

He was being drawn into the madness of the whole idea. The desire to spend time with her was strong. How could something that felt so right, be wrong? They would have separate rooms; all they would share would be companionship, he reasoned. He might finally discover what had been troubling her. He might be able to help her. He wanted to help her ... needed to help her. “Right, you’re on. Let’s go.”

CHAPTER 18

Diana heard the phone but she had just got into the bath and she did not want to get out. She guessed it wouldn't be anything important. These days nothing much of importance happened. When Andrew had been alive there was always something, especially before his retirement; emergency meetings; distressed parishioners, important services.

She sank up to her neck in bubbles and stuck a leg in the air, revelling in the smoothness of her skin. There was something to be said for an evening of pampering.

The phone rang again. Two calls in quick succession. Maybe it *was* something important. No, it couldn't be. She sponged her face and laid her head against the back of the bath. For some reason she began to think of Mary Briggs. It reminded her of Andrew's decline. She felt a lump in her throat and wondered if she would miss him forever.

The water was cooling. The phone rang again. This time she stood up and grabbed a towel. "Hello." She waited but there was nothing. "Hello," she repeated as she dripped onto the carpet. She heard what sounded like a sob and then a voice thick with grief. "She's gone."

"Tom, is that you?"

"Mum had a stroke and while we were waiting for the ambulance to arrive. She died, just like that, sitting in her chair."

"I'm so sorry. Are the children with you?"

"No ... there's no-one here now. Can I come round ... I need to get away from the house."

She glanced down at the damp towel. She checked her hair

in the mirror and noticed streaks of mascara tracing her laughter lines. She licked a finger and tried to remove the smudges. "Of course you can," she said.

"I'll see you in about ten minutes."

She hurried into the bedroom to get dressed. A pair of trousers and a nice top would do. She returned the towel to the bathroom and pulled the plug on the de-bubbled water with one hand while she spritzed perfume with the other. Poor Tom, he sounded so upset. She hoped he would hear comforting words from someone who had been his mother's friend and who was his friend's mother; Andrew had been so good with words. He would have known what to say to make a difference. This was her chance to make a difference. She felt her cheeks redden in embarrassment at her inadequacy and barely had time to compose herself before the doorbell buzzed.

Her heart went out to him as he stood on the threshold waiting to be encouraged inside, dishevelled, broken, his eyes red from grief and she knew instinctively what was necessary. "You poor love," she said taking his arm and drawing him towards her. "It must have been awful for you."

"It was."

"Come and sit down. I'll pour you a whisky."

He let her lead him into the compact sitting room and accepted the glass of whisky she offered. "Andrew's favourite tipple," she said. "He reckoned it cured everything from arthritis to a broken heart."

"The house seems empty without her."

"It will."

"She went so quickly; one minute she was there and then ... nothing."

"That's hard for you, but it's by far the best way. You wouldn't have wanted her to suffer."

"No." He gulped another mouthful of whisky. "I don't know what I'm going to do about the funeral. She wouldn't discuss it."

She re-filled his glass and poured one for herself. "I can help you with that if you like."

"Would you?"

"Of course I will; it's hard enough having to deal with all the formalities when you can think straight and you won't be doing that for a while. There's nothing much you can do until you get the death certificate anyway. It will give you time to let people know, talk to the children, work out how you want it to be."

His hand trembled as he raised the glass to his lips again. He attached the other one to it like a crampon. "Cry if you want to," Diana said. "I won't mind. I've plenty of tissues."

She held out the box but he shook his head and swallowed some more whisky down. "I'm sorry to lean on you like this but I didn't know where else to turn."

"Don't worry about it. I'm glad you thought of me. Have you had something to eat?"

"I'm not hungry. It was awful when the undertakers came to take her away," he said, his face twisting with emotion. He put the glass down for a moment while he controlled himself. She moved across to the sofa and put an arm about his shoulders. "Where are the children?"

"Harry and Jim had a squash tournament organised. They wanted to go and I thought it was a good idea. Colette went over to Janine's. She's been very good about everything. I didn't expect her support but she got on well with Mum even after the divorce. At least I know who to contact about the will. She made a new one last year. I'll call Jon tomorrow."

"You'll have to leave it until Tuesday. He's not here this weekend."

"It's going to be a funny weekend for us. I'll have to let the carer know she won't be needed. There's so much to sort out."

"I'm afraid there is but you don't have to do it all at once;

give yourself time to take it in."

He drained the glass. "Thanks, Diana ... for the whisky, for listening, for everything."

"I'm happy to listen if it helps. I know what it's like, dealing with death."

"I'd better get back." He glanced around the room, noticing for the first time how much she had crammed into the space. "You've got a lot of stuff in here ... are you sure I can't help you to dispose of some of it?"

"I don't think any of it is worth selling at auction."

"That vase over there," he said. "Where did it come from?"

"It's awful isn't it? It's been in our family for years. It belonged to my grandmother. My grandfather was a merchant seaman. Their house was full of souvenirs he brought back from all over the place. I should have taken it down to the British Heart Foundation when we moved but Andrew liked it and somehow, when he'd gone, I couldn't do it. Are you going to report me to the taste police?"

"Do you mind if I take a look?"

"Be my guest."

The vase stood about four feet tall on its wooden stand. He crouched down beside the embossed dragons and ran his fingers over the delicate crackled glaze, lifting it from its stand with both arms like the world's strongest man as he searched for marks on the base. "It's old ... Chinese. Do you know how much this could be worth?"

"Ooh probably five pounds in a charity shop."

"You're way out. Everything oriental is hot at the moment. The Chinese bid online. It could raise thousands."

"Don't be silly."

"I'm being serious. I think you should consider it."

"Yes. Well, I'll think about it but if I agree, I don't want anyone to know it's mine. I'd be so embarrassed if I had to take it home again especially after the painting was such a spectacular flop."

"You were just unlucky there. It went in the end. I don't think you'll have any trouble finding interested bidders this time. Trust me."

CHAPTER 19

Daisy awoke to a fierce knocking on Saturday. Early morning visitors usually meant trouble. She sniffed the air as she grabbed her glasses from the bed-side table ... no smoke. Not a fire, then. She wondered if there had been a break-in at church and then remembered that Fr. Jon was there. It wasn't up to her any more ... but he wasn't there. He was away. She snatched the woollen throw lying at the foot of her bed, draping it toga-like over her night dress before rushing to open the door. She was astonished to find Rachel standing there, coat-less and wind-swept, her face contorted with emotion. Anger ... frustration ... grief ... she could not tell which. "Rachel ... what on earth's happened?"

"Can I come in? I've been driving about for most of the night."

"You must be frozen," Daisy let the toga slip and draped it round Rachel's shoulders instead. "Come through to the kitchen it's the warmest room first thing."

"What time is it, I've lost track."

"It must be about half-past six. The heating's just come on ... I'll make us a drink."

"I'm absolutely livid," Rachel said.

"What's going on?"

"John's left me."

Daisy whisked round to face her leaving water to cascade over the kettle into the sink. "No ... not after all these years ... has he had a mid-life crisis?"

"It's worse than that," she went on as Daisy mopped up splashes and plugged in the kettle. "There's someone else."

"Oh dear," Daisy said, truly horrified. She had always thought of John as a rather unattractive character with his hooked nose and generous belly.

"And that's not all."

"How do you mean?"

"He's got a family with her."

Daisy sank onto a chair ignoring the plumes of steam issuing from the kettle. "Rachel, that's just appalling."

"You've no idea what a shock it was. He said we couldn't have children while his work took him away so much. He knew I wanted children ... I told him enough times. I asked him to change jobs. We had row upon row over it. He said it was too soon; he wasn't earning enough; it wasn't fair to ask me to do everything ... you'd be amazed at the excuses he dreamed up. I know he was away a lot but I would have managed."

"Of course you would."

"I tried to persuade him. We had the same conversation every Christmas ... I hate Christmas," Rachel said. "What gets me is that while he was saying all these things to me, he was making babies with someone else."

"I don't know what to say ... I wonder how he explained that to her, being somewhere else at Christmas, I mean.

"I wonder if she knows what a liar he is."

"It's very sad ... but there were compensations."

"The holidays, you mean ..."

"Yes ... but what a traitor."

"I called him worse than that. I threw his precious wine all over him, too."

"Good for you," Daisy said. "Where is he now?"

"He's gone ... packed a suitcase and cleared off ... just like the little weasel he is."

"What's going to happen?"

"I told him I wanted a divorce before he could say that's what *he* wanted. I'll cite adultery and I'm going to take him to the cleaners," she said, all her chins wobbling in righteous indignation. "The flat's in my name fortunately. He insisted on that for tax purposes. At least I'll have somewhere to live and I've got my own bank account. I'm not worried about money; the council pension's enough to live on but I'm not going to let him get away with it."

"Quite right; what a shame Fr. Jon's away. You could do with talking to him about it."

"I'm talking to you. It's probably better I can't talk to him right now. I feel so angry. I don't want him to see me in this state. I've wasted the best years of my life on that man ... for nothing."

"How could you not have known there was something going on?"

"I have absolutely no idea. I've gone over and over it in my mind since he told me. You read about it in the papers. I always thought wives who didn't know what was happening in their husbands' lives must be a bit thick but I didn't have a clue what he was up to. He's always travelled but he's never missed a birthday or Christmas, like I said; when his mother was alive, we went over there each year and I had to put up with all her nonsense ... for twenty years I did that."

"I can't understand it."

"Neither can I ... we didn't live in each other's pockets, he played a lot of golf. I had my bridge but still ..." she hesitated, staring at Daisy's face "I didn't know you wore glasses, Daisy."

"I haven't had a chance to sort out my contacts. I don't usually entertain before breakfast."

"I'm sorry to land on you like this."

"I don't mind at all."

"I wonder what the others will say."

"Well ... it will be headline news for a few days and then everything will settle down again. It's probably best if you tell them straight away rather than let them imagine what's been going on."

"You're right. I will. I know ... I'm going to have a party."

"Are you sure that's a good idea?"

"I think it's a very good idea. I'm not going to hide away. I've done nothing wrong and I'm not really upset. I'll admit I was shocked at first and very, very angry, I'm still angry but over the years I've learned how to live without him. I won't miss him one bit," she said with excessive bravado. "He's welcome to his bit on the side and she's welcome to him. We can enjoy his wine."

Ben shuffled into the kitchen and switched on the kettle, mulling over the strange phenomenon he had experienced the night before as he kept watch over the town in his eyrie.

Bella emerged from her room in a silk kimono, yawning and scratching her head. Her hair looked like shredded wheat and her knees creaked as she tottered down the stairs. "Have you made the tea," she asked.

"It's in the pot," he said, blowing at the top of the steaming mug he had already poured out for himself.

"Hairdresser this morning," she said. "I need to get these roots done."

"I saw something last night," he began.

"You're always seeing things," she said dismissively. "Yesterday it was a strange man loitering in town. No-one else saw him."

"How do you know?"

"Joan Drabble called round while you were out. If anyone had seen anything suspicious she would have known about it."

"Well I know I saw Rachel Meeks driving round in all that rain last night."

"Did you ..." she said adding a second teaspoon of sugar to her tea.

"She drove past here *four* times."

"How many whiskies did you have after I went to bed?"

"Just the one ... she was driving like a bat out of hell," he said staring out of the window. "She was lucky not to have crashed."

"I'll get the bacon in the pan."

"Don't you think it's a bit odd?"

"Everything that woman does is a bit odd, if you ask me. What time was it anyway?"

"Three-ish."

"Now, that *is* odd. You should have been in bed."

"What do you think she was doing?"

"I don't know and I really don't care."

"The vicar's still away."

"Good."

"Thyme's lights weren't on last night either ... I think she's still away too."

"I'm even less interested in her. There aren't any tomatoes," she said peering into the bottom of the fridge. "I might speak to Marion about Rachel, though. Remind me to phone her later."

"What do you think?" Angela Reedman said as she held up her latest creation to show her husband.

"Hmm ... very nice," he said.

She shuffled through the box of finished cards. "Have I done enough, do you think?" she said, more to herself than to him.

"You can never do enough," he said. "How much are you charging?"

"We-e-ell, I thought two pounds fifty each. When you take into account my time and what I've had to buy to make them, that's fair."

"And how many have you made?"

"About thirty ..."

"Thirty at two pounds fifty each ..."

"That's seventy-five pounds, but only if they all sell."

"Make it three pounds a pop."

"No-one's going to pay that."

"They're hand-made."

"I know how much people round here are prepared to pay," she said, "Two pounds fifty each."

"I don't know why you bothered to ask me."

"I didn't. You asked me ..."

"Never mind that, I've got to work out where all the tables are going."

"I thought Daisy usually organises the tables."

"Well, I'm doing it. She's got enough on her plate with all the other things she has to organise."

"Have you told her?"

"I don't need to. I'm on the committee."

"You're not in charge, Owen."

"I know all about getting the best from people; I've organised events all my life."

"Not church bazaars you haven't. Let Daisy get on with it. Don't interfere."

"You don't know what you're talking about. Those women need someone to take charge."

Angela sighed. "Have you sorted out the Organometer?"

"It's all in hand."

"When can we have Fr. Jon round for a meal?"

"He's away."

"Well, obviously not this weekend."

"What about next Friday?"

"How about Sunday lunch, invite him round after church. Georgia's more likely to be free then."

"You're wasting your time, woman. Daisy said he's not looking for a wife."

"He might not *think* he is," Angela said. "He hasn't met

Georgia yet."

Neil stepped back to get a better look at the windows of his sister's house. They were all as dark and unrevealing as an off-line monitor. He rang the bell again and then felt in his pocket for the spare key she had left with him. "It's only me," he called as he walked through to the kitchen. He noticed straight away that the case wasn't there. There was an upside down cup and saucer standing on the draining board along with a few teaspoons dropped in a random pattern. The washing machine was empty, the back door was locked. He knew instinctively that the house was empty too, but it didn't prevent him from walking into the hall to call her again. He glanced up at the landing. The loft hatch was shut.

"How is she?" Chantal asked when he returned to the car.

"She wasn't there."

"How do you mean?"

"As in, she wasn't there," he said. "She must have gone away with Jill. She said she might."

"It's odd that she didn't let you know."

"She mentioned it the other day ... said it would give us a break. I expect she'll text later. We'd better get back to Amy."

"Alice is there."

"I know but she'll be on the computer."

"I'm sure they'll be fine. I thought we could go and check out some more bathroom fittings."

"We can't do anything until the money comes through."

"I know but I haven't had a chance to go to the show-room in Linchester yet. There might be a special offer on. It would be silly not to make sure we're not missing out on a bargain."

"Ok but I'll text Alice first."

CHAPTER 20

Monday morning in the Sykes household was the usual scramble to find lost homework and scrape together a healthy lunch for Alice. Neil's work had been put on hold while Amy was ill and while he didn't resent the time spent looking after her he was desperate to get back to his normal routine. "I've put an apple in your lunch-box," he said to Alice as she packed her school bag. She pulled a face. "I don't want to find it rolling around under your bed like the last one."

"I don't want lunch," she said.

"You won't be able to concentrate this afternoon if you don't eat it," Chantal said. "Hurry up. I need to be there early today."

"Are you happy with your speech now?" Neil asked.

"I don't know. I'm dreading this governors' meeting. I'm sure some of the figures don't add up. That's why I want to be in school early. I need to ask Moira to check them for me. I couldn't be a school bursar. It would drive me mad. Are you ready now Alice?"

Alice tossed her hair out of her eyes. "I've been ready ages."

"Come on, then ... bye Neil, wish me luck."

He kissed both of her cheeks. "You won't need it, but good luck anyway." He walked them to the door and waved them off, glad to be on his own for five minutes. He stacked the dishwasher, loaded the washing machine and went upstairs to see if Amy was awake. She was curled up in bed, her thumb suspiciously near her mouth. He tapped on the door and she rolled over, stretched and rubbed her eyes. "Hi Dad."

"Alice and Mum have gone ... breakfast's on the table," he

said.

"Five minutes ..." she said sleepily.

"Ok ... I'm going to check my messages and then I'll be back to sort you out."

"Where *is* Thyme?" she asked as he dotted the last of her spots with calamine lotion.

"She's gone away with Jill."

"I texted her but she hasn't replied."

"There ... that's you done. No new ones today. Hasn't she? I'll text her too, tell her she's out of order."

Amy giggled. "When can I go back to school? I'm missing loads of work."

"You can go back as soon as all the scabs have dried up; you're infectious until then. It won't be long now ... perhaps the end of the week."

"Chicken pox is rank," she said.

"I know. You can come to the supermarket with me in a minute if you like."

She sighed. "But I'll have to sit in the car ... I'd rather stay here."

"I'll bring you a cake to cheer you up."

"You mean one of Jill's cakes?"

"If that's what you want."

"Yes, please."

"Your wish is my command."

"The phone's ringing."

"I'll take it downstairs and then I'm going," he said. "Get dressed and don't answer the door while I'm out."

"Can I go on your computer?" she called.

"Yes but don't change any of the settings." He picked up the phone. "Charne ... what's up?"

"Have you been to the supermarket yet?"

"I'm on my way, why?"

"I forgot to tell you, Alice needs some things for home

economics."

"She's given me a list."

"Ah ... so the message has got through at last. Is Amy ok?"

"Amy's fine. She must be feeling a lot better, she's missing school. I said I'd buy her a cake to cheer her up."

"You spoil her."

"Everyone needs a bit of spoiling when they're ill ... is there anything else, or can I get on?"

"No, that's it. I'm just off to the meeting. See you tonight."

When he reached Quality Cakes, Gemma was standing at the till. The door was open allowing the queue to stretch right out onto the pavement, carrying with it the scent of freshly baked rolls. He decided to wait. Amy would be disappointed if he returned without the promised cake. The queue moved slowly forward and his mouth watered as he glanced up and down the display at the batches of almond slices, sticky Danish pastries and a tray full of freshly-baked doughnuts dusted with sugar. He was just admiring a chocolate gateau gyrating slowly round on a revolving cake stand when he realised someone else had appeared behind the counter to help out. He stared at her, rooted to the spot. Jill smiled at him. "Hi Neil, how's Thyme," she said.

"I thought she was with you."

"No, I haven't seen her for a few days."

"Well she was fine when I dropped her off at home on Friday," he said hastily covering his astonishment with a grin. "Could I have a Victoria sandwich please?"

He walked out of the shop considering his next move. If Thyme wasn't with Jill, who was she with? Her message had been short and to the point informing him that she was ok and would be home on Tuesday. She hadn't said anything about where she was, or who she was with. She couldn't have driven anywhere with her leg pinned and it would be difficult travelling by train.

He had to tell Chantal. He fingered his phone and then remembered about the meeting. He would have to wait until she came home that evening.

"What do you think Thyme's doing?" Amy said as she sat making friendship bracelets at the kitchen table while Neil prepared lunch.

He had been wondering the same thing himself, had thought of little else since he had returned home, but he didn't want to alarm her by revealing that. "She's probably having something to eat," he said.

"Where has she gone?"

"I don't know."

"I hope her leg doesn't hurt too much."

He glanced across at her, noting her troubled expression. "You don't need to worry about Thyme. She's doing very well."

"When will she be back?"

"Soon."

"Da – a – d," she said.

He looked up from the cheese he was watching bubble under the grill to see her perched on one of the stools staring out of the window onto the road. "What is it?"

"There's a man outside."

He went back to contemplating cheese. "It's a free world," he said.

"But he's staring at our house."

"I expect he's admiring the new gates. He'll be ringing the bell in a minute to ask where we bought them."

"Maybe," she said doubtfully. "He's still there," she said. "I don't like him."

He switched off the grill, removed the dish of cauliflower cheese and joined her at the window.

"Where is he? I can't see anyone," he said flipping the oven gloves over his shoulder.

She braced herself against the work-top to peep over his head.

"Don't know," she said. "He's gone."

"Well, that's that then ... do you want your lunch now?"

He spent the rest of the day trying to amuse her but she knew his heart wasn't in it. "It's your turn, Dad ..." she said for the fourth time in a row as they played Scrabble. "Dad ... it's you ... come on."

"Sorry ... a, n, d ... that's the best I can do," he said.

He took the last two tiles from the bag and waited for her to take her turn.

"S, n, o, w ... double word score ... I've won, I've won," she shouted, bouncing about in glee.

"Oh, very good Amy ... now, why don't you go and watch a DVD? I'll put this lot away."

As soon as Chantal arrived with Alice, he hurried her into the kitchen and shut the door so that the children wouldn't hear them. "What's the matter, Neil?"

"When I went to fetch Amy's cake I saw Jill in the cake shop."

"So? That's where she works."

"She can't be in two places at once."

"Oh ... I see. You mean she's not with Thyme ... hmm."

"Should we phone the police?"

"No, of course not, you've had a text from her haven't you, so she must be all right."

"Yes, but who is she with? She couldn't have arranged a trip on her own the state she's in at the moment."

"She didn't say who she was with."

"Nope."

"Well, she doesn't want you to know ... that's it. It would explain everything. That's why she didn't want to talk. She's in a new relationship and she doesn't want to say anything until she's sure it's going somewhere. You have to respect her privacy."

"How do you work that out? Surely if she had a new man he would have visited her in hospital."

"How do you know he didn't? You weren't with her twenty-four seven."

"I'm still worried. What if he's a bit iffy? She's got a lot to lose if he's after her money. What if she has another accident?"

"Neil, you're being silly. She'll be back tomorrow and for sure there are doctors and hospitals wherever she is ... open this," she said presenting him with a bottle of Prosecco. "We both need a drink."

CHAPTER 21

Thyme had spent Saturday resting in her room while Jon got on with his work; they had met only briefly for meals and managed a modicum of small talk. Sunday passed in much the same way apart from a stroll in the hotel grounds. By Monday she felt less tired and more sociable despite spending an uncomfortable night with her leg. She shuffled out of bed and peered through the curtains to see mossy boulders set amongst gorse and cropped grass. There was a slight movement in the surrounding trees and as she watched, a fawn appeared, ears pricked, dark eyes checking for danger. It picked its way through the bracken on slender legs. A dog barked some way off and the animal disappeared as suddenly as it had arrived. At the same time she heard a soft tap on the door. "Hold on a minute." She grabbed a hoodie and pulled it over her pyjama top. "Come in."

"I didn't know if you'd be awake," he said as he hesitated half in and half out of the room. "Are you having breakfast?"

"I'm starving," she said. "Give me half an hour. I'll meet you down there."

"It's only eight thirty. There's no rush."

It took her longer than expected to get dressed. She had to sit down several times to catch her breath. It was well after nine when the lift opened to urge her out onto the ground floor.

She saw Jon relaxing in one of the easy chairs in the hall. He looked different without his dog collar and with his hair wet from the shower. No-one would have guessed he was a vicar in the open-neck shirt and cashmere sweater he had chosen to wear with his jeans. He had been reading a newspaper but he glanced up when he heard the lift arrive. He moved swiftly over to help her out. "Thanks. It would be easier without the crutches," she said.

"Would it? I fell off the bike a few years back and broke my ankle; I know what it's like to have to hobble about. You don't want to try walking without them," he said. "Where shall we sit today?"

About half the tables were occupied. "I don't mind ... anywhere ... here," she said choosing a table with a good view of the double-glazed panorama. "I saw a deer out there earlier."

"We're really out in the wilds," he said. "I'm glad you suggested it. I wanted to go somewhere isolated, as far from mobile networks as possible so I could get on with the book but I've still got reception."

"You could just turn it off," she said.

He grinned. "Don't worry, I have. What are you having this morning?"

"Porridge," she said.

"I fancy a full English ... it's no good trying to write on an empty stomach ... are you feeling more rested today?

"Sorry I slept most of yesterday." she said.

"It's fine. I managed to get a lot done ... I'll go and find the waitress." He was back with a rack of toast. "I thought we could start on this. What are you planning to do after breakfast?"

"Not much. I won't interfere with your writing, if that's what you mean. Pretend I'm not here. I saw a book corner by reception last night. I could catch up on some reading."

"I thought I'd get started straight after breakfast."

"Here it is ... that looks good," she said eyeing up the bacon.

"Do you want some?"

"No, I'll stick with my porridge, thanks."

Eating took over from speaking for a while. "We could have lunch together," he said as his plate emptied.

"That would be good."

"I'll tell reception we'll need something to eat at lunch-time ..."

"... and this evening," she added. "I seem to have got my appetite back."

"You're definitely on the mend, then," he said, settling his knife and fork neatly together on the plate. He stood up and dropped the newspaper onto her lap. "Here, you may as well have this. I'd better crack on. See you twelve-ish."

She finished her toast and glanced around the room ... there was no-one left. The young couple she had noticed earlier dressed for some serious walking in knee breeches and thick woollen socks, had gone. Everyone had deserted her. It was time she texted Neil again. Her previous message had been deliberately brief. She tapped out a reassurance that all was well and swung her leg out sideways from the table, taking hold of the crutches Jon had propped against an empty chair nearby. She picked up the newspaper and hobbled over to the reception desk. "Can you recommend a good taxi service?" she said. "I thought I might go out later."

"There's not much to see," the girl said. "Just the old castle and a few touristy shops; you'd have to drive a wee bit further to find some decent shops ... can't your friend take you?"

"He's trying to work. I don't want to disturb him ... I quite like the castle."

"You've been there before?"

"A long time ago ... I was here with my aunt."

"I don't think it's changed much. We usually recommend the Red Line Cabs; I've got one of their cards here."

"Thanks. This hotel hasn't changed much either."

"I wouldn't know. I've only worked here for six months. The owners like to think of it as a home from home."

"That's just how it feels. Is it alright if I borrow one of your books?"

"Help yourself. We've lit the fire in the lounge. You'll be quiet in there. Everyone else has gone out. Would you like me to bring you morning tea later?"

"That would be great, thanks ... I'll read for a bit and then I'll go out."

Jon clicked 'save' and gave himself a virtual pat on the back. All the recipes were finished. He had added his special tips and some short cuts to the more complicated methods. He had written the introduction. All he had left to add was an explanation as to why he had picked those particular dishes. He reckoned another day's work should tie it all up.

He was pleased Thyme seemed much happier. She hadn't volunteered any further information about what had been troubling her but he was content to take it at her pace. He was hoping she might feel comfortable enough to open up to him before they left Scotland. She hadn't suggested visiting her son ... he thought she might be waiting for him to say something and decided to mention it later. He reckoned that now they were across the border it would be a shame not to.

He left his lap-top to do some updating and strolled back downstairs. The dining room was empty. He tried the lounge. It was a low-ceilinged room with a large fireplace. Logs were smouldering in a basket on the grate. The carpet was a neutral brown but as in the dining room there were tartan lampshades on the wall lights and also a tartan throw on one of the armchairs. A tray of tea-things sat on the coffee table. Thyme was asleep on the couch, the borrowed book upside down on the floor beside her. As he hesitated by the door, she must have sensed his presence. Her eyelids flew open and she sat up. "What time is it?" she said.

"It's one o'clock."

"I must have been asleep for hours."

"Don't worry about it. You need your sleep."

"I had a bad night," she said. "I couldn't find a comfortable place for my leg and I didn't want to get up to take some more painkillers."

"Are you still having lunch or do you want to doze?"

"I'm awake now. I'll come with you," she said hoisting herself to her feet on her good leg before she grabbed the crutches. "I don't want to waste the afternoon as well. How did you get on with the book?"

"Very well ... another session should see it done and then I'll need someone to proof read it."

"I'd be happy to do that."

"Are you sure?"

"I am a librarian."

"Oh yes ... I'd forgotten ... well, if you really don't mind ..."

"I'd like to help. You drove me all the way up here."

"I was going to ask when you'd like to visit your son. I don't mind taking you. We haven't much time left now." Only a few of the tables in the dining room had been laid. Scottish reels jigged away in the background. "There's nothing like bagpipes to set the scene," he said. He had been expecting to raise a smile but her face was serious as she pulled a chair from the nearest table and sat down. He caught the crutches as they fell from her hands. "Are you all right?"

She glanced at the menu. "Soup," she said.

"We'll have the soup, please," he said as the waitress hovered.

"There's something I need to say to you," she said her eyes fixed on the tartan table-cloth.

"You hate bagpipe music," he joked and then realised she was not laughing. Could this be the moment he had been waiting for ... he hoped his flippant attitude hadn't dissuaded her from confiding in him. "I'm sorry," he said. "Carry on. I'm listening."

"I haven't told anyone else."

"You know I won't pass it on."

She turned to him, her eyes bright with tears. "I don't have a son," she said.

"Now you've lost me," he said. "What do you mean?"

It's simple enough," she said. "I don't have a son, that's it."

"You don't have a son," he repeated as if he was trying to make sense of a cryptic clue. "You told me he was in Scotland; I thought that was why you were here."

"He is ... this is where I left him," she said, picking tiny bobbles of wool from the sleeves of her jumper.

"I'm sorry but you're going to have to explain. I don't get it."

Two bowls of steaming carrot and coriander arrived along with a basket of bread rolls. She took one of the rolls and proceeded to tear it apart bit by bit until there was a mosaic of crumbs decorating her plate while he waited for more. "I had a son once ... but now I don't," she said.

"Is this why you were in the church ... what you needed help with?" he said. "He died."

"I killed him," she said. "There's a subtle difference."

"You killed him?" She nodded. He felt as if a glass screen had sprung up between them. He had a sense that if he touched it, touched her, it would shatter and with it, all his hopes. The ground he had made up between them would be lost. Was she capable of such an act? "Help me Lord," was his silent prayer as she sipped soup from the spoon and kept her eyes glued to the bowl. After a few minutes he decided he had to say something. "I don't believe you."

"Take me to the castle after lunch," she said quietly. "I'll explain there."

CHAPTER 22

They exchanged few comments on the short drive to the castle. The easy camaraderie they had shared over the past few days had evaporated. Jon restricted himself to remarks about the scenery and Thyme either nodded or shook her head as necessary.

He brought the car to a halt in the road running alongside the ruin. Crows picked about in the boulders that littered the grass blanketing the foundations of the once sturdy stronghold. He glanced up at the arrow slits on the crumbling stone face and noticed a couple of magpies stalking the allure like mediaeval archers. “One for sorrow, two for joy,” he said as they soared above the roofless walls cackling like crones. He switched off the engine. “Do you want to get out?”

She wound down the window to cool her cheeks and breathe in the mossy air. “No ... Aunt Lal loved this place,” she began. “She brought me up here when it all went wrong.”

“Is this about Ollie? I know about your break-up. Ben came to see me.”

“I didn’t break up with him. He broke up with me. He’d been applying for jobs in New Zealand but keeping it quiet. I was so excited when I found out I was pregnant. It’s what I’d always wanted, to make my own little family after our dysfunctional one, but when I told him about the baby he went mad. He didn’t want to be part of a family. It wasn’t in his plan. He didn’t even want me to go to New Zealand with him. The minute I realised that and the fact that our engagement had been a farce I went into melt-down. I couldn’t stop crying for days. My mum was worse than useless. I tried to talk to his mum but she didn't want to know."

"I gathered that from what she said to me. Did she know about the baby?"

"Oh ... she knew."

"I went to see her last week. She didn't mention it. I don't think Ben knows."

"He wasn't there when I called round to see her. She said it was my fault Ollie was going away. She wouldn't listen when I tried to tell her the truth. I left it a few days and then I wrote to her and explained everything. She didn't reply. I wrote again, I was desperate ... still no reply. In the end Aunt Lal came to my rescue. She brought me up here and we decided that an abortion would be best. Time was ticking and I'd reached eighteen weeks by then. She found a clinic in Edinburgh. I had to give birth to my baby. It was a boy. I called him Matthew. He was so small ... so quiet ... not moving ... like a wax doll with his little eyes closed. I wanted to cuddle him but he was whisked away ..." the colour had drained from her cheeks; her hands gripped each other so tightly that he thought her knuckles would break through the transparent skin.

"... I made a life for him; that was aunt Lal's suggestion. She said to buy him a present each year on his birthday and donate it to charity. I bought the presents but I couldn't bear to part with them. I wrapped each one, wrote the labels and put them away in a suitcase. She didn't know. That suitcase has travelled everywhere with me. It's in the attic of the house I'm renting now. You saw his last gift."

"The parcel you had with you in Sue's Place."

She nodded. "It was the day ... his actual birthday." She pulled a tissue from her pocket and dried the tears coursing down her cheeks. "Neil must have seen me coming down from the attic when he called the same day but he didn't ask what I was doing. I wish he had. I nearly told him but I didn't have the courage. I was scared of what he might say. I'm such a coward."

"I wish you'd said something to me."

"I couldn't. I didn't know you then."

"You've kept all this inside for years. I'm amazed you didn't share it with anyone."

"Only Aunt Lal ... talking about Matt seemed to help. I'd see children in the street of about the same age and imagine how he might have looked. As he got older I planned girlfriends for him, trips abroad. I invented a virtual Matt life. I knew it wasn't real, Aunt Lal knew it wasn't real. It was our secret. She played along with it but I wanted her to tell me I was being ridiculous. I needed her permission to let him go. She didn't see it. I suppose she thought it would be dangerous to rock the boat. She knew how vulnerable I was. It wasn't until she died that I realised I had to say something to someone else, to try and deal with the terrible guilt I felt.

I couldn't talk to Neil. He would know I'd been lying to him for all those years. If my mother had told him what had happened, it would have been so much easier. She told him Ollie and I had split up but she didn't mention the baby. He was a little person, Jon. She wanted to pretend he'd never existed. I couldn't do that. Did she think it would all miraculously disappear if we didn't talk about it ... about him?"

He understood that her actions had tipped her to the brink of insanity. He could see her remorse was genuine. He wanted to find a way to comfort her but he didn't know what to say; all he could do was shake his head. "You disapprove, don't you?"

"It's not for me to approve or disapprove."

"But you do, don't you?" she persisted. "I can't bear any more pretending. That's what's been preying on my mind. I can't get it out of my head. No-one knows what a horrible person I am. Everyone's been treating me as if I'm normal, nice, sensible, kind. What mother would kill her own baby ... I'm a monster, aren't I?" She searched his face for the truth.

He was torn between his beliefs and her visible distress. He knew it demanded a response from him. "I'm so sorry. It must have been awful for you." He did not re-coil from her as a person. He accepted her reasons for terminating the life of her child. Part of him understood the desperation of a naive nineteen year old abandoned by her fiancé and seeing no future for herself or her baby without him, but the sticking point was his fundamental conviction that abortion was wrong. "You're not a monster; I can't deny I would have handled things differently and I won't condone what you've done but I can't judge you. I know how much you've suffered and how much you regret what you did but spending the rest of your life paying for it isn't right either. Neil won't hold this against you and he won't love you any less if he's who I think he is; did you know he rang me? He's worried about you."

"So that's why you turned up on Friday."

"I would have come anyway. I was waiting for you to call and when you didn't I wanted to check you were ok before I went away, whatever you'd done ... or thought you'd done."

"You don't hate me?" she asked in a small voice.

"I don't hate you." He wanted to say that in spite of her revelation he thought he was falling in love with her. Her hand was lying right next to his. It would have been so easy to take it and hold it tight but he couldn't let that happen. She trusted him. To take advantage of her vulnerability at that moment would have been wrong. His head had become a cocktail shaker with emotions and fundamental beliefs crashing against each other like ice cubes in a highball.

This was the kind of dilemma he had never envisaged for himself. If he was counselling others he would try to be fair, to separate the practical from the emotional but he could not do that for himself. His confusion troubled him; he couldn't reveal that to her; he needed to clear his head but he couldn't do that either. This was not about him. She needed more than the words he had given already. He had to feel his way and go with his instincts, trust he would get it right. “Did you consider adoption?”

“We discussed it ...”

“And ...?”

“I had a friend at school who was adopted. She always felt second-best, like her real mum didn’t want her. I didn’t want Matt to feel that way all his life. You can never tell what sort of people are going to adopt. He could have been lucky, had a happy childhood but what if they had been unkind to him? I wouldn’t have been able to rescue him. I couldn’t take the risk. Aunt Lal said it was for me to decide. She didn’t want to influence me either way. In the end I thought terminating the pregnancy was the only way we could both be happy; the irony of it is that it didn’t make me happy at all. I was heartbroken. I couldn’t get over what I’d done. I didn’t want to forget my son.”

“That’s such a sad story.”

“Aunt Lal thought it would be for the best. I know she was only trying to help but nothing helped. I couldn’t concentrate. I couldn’t sleep. She marched me off to see the doctor; I tried sleeping pills, happy pills, homeopathic remedies ... nothing touched the emotional pain. You know, sometimes I felt like a pressure cooker with all these feelings building up inside me; I was close to exploding when we met at Sue’s Place.”

“Why didn’t you try counselling?”

“I would have had to give away my secret to a stranger. I couldn’t do it; that was all I had left of him. The church was my last hope and when that didn’t help, I didn’t know where to turn. I felt so alone.”

“Well, you’re not alone now.”

She stared at him, eyes like discs of liquorice in her ashen cheeks. “And what would your God say?”

“He’d say that he loves you and that we’re all sinners. We’ll be forgiven if our repentance is genuine as yours is. You've suffered enough, Thyme. God isn't punishing you. Matt's safe with him. He's forgiven you. You need to forgive yourself and you need to tell Neil."

CHAPTER 23

Diana did not have time to miss Jon over the weekend. She had spent most of it helping Tom and his family sort through Mary's clothes and trying to decide what she should do about the vase. On Tuesday she was with Daisy. "It's so sad about Mary," she said.

"I called round with a card."

"Tom's in pieces."

"It was the best thing for her, for everyone," Daisy said. "He'll see that when he's recovered from the shock. It's too awful watching someone deteriorate and have to go into hospital or a hospice. She was only going to get worse. We should go to the funeral."

"Yes. Nothing's been arranged as yet. I asked him to let me know when they have a date."

"When Jon's back he'll sort out the arrangements."

"I haven't tried to contact him. He wanted a complete break to finish the book."

"I know."

"If we manage to sort out a date for the book launch at least we'll have some positive news for him."

"It will have to be after the Easter fair," Daisy said. "I can't organise anything until that's over."

"So what are we saying, beginning of May?"

"I think so ... how about the first weekend in May? If the weather's good we could have drinks in the garden and the book signing in the conservatory."

"That sounds lovely, Daisy, let's hope we make a lot of sales."

"We've still got a long way to go with the fund-raising."

"Tom told me he's had an offer for the painting at the reserve price."

"Are you going to accept?"

"I think so. I want to speak to Jon first. He's coming round for a meal when he gets home. I'll ask him then. He might want to put it back in the auction, try for more."

"He won't turn his nose up at fifteen hundred, surely ... a bird in the hand and all that."

"I agree but I still want to ask him."

"Do you know who made the offer?"

"It was some builder over Linchester way."

"Not Mike Chisholm."

"That was it."

"I know him. He gave me a quote for my new kitchen. His brother's married to Isobel Flynn's daughter ... a bit of a rough diamond but he does a good job at a fair price."

"Perhaps he might pay more if he knows where the money's going."

"He won't and for heaven's sake tell Tom not to mention it. He's very anti-church. His daughter's training to be a priest and he's not happy about it."

"What a shame. I thought all that had changed ... I considered the church myself, years ago."

"You didn't ..."

"Yes ... but it went no further than the considering. I would have been going against the male hierarchy then and it was all too much; much worse than it is now. Anyway I got pregnant with Jon and that was that. I wouldn't have had the time to devote to all the studying; being a vicar's wife and a mum was busy enough for me."

She didn't want to prolong their meeting. She knew if they got chatting, the topic of the vase might slip out by accident and she was not about to advertise her latest fund-raising scheme. If she decided to sell and it raised a fortune, all well and good; if not ... well, it would go back to its place by the wall and no-one would be any the wiser. "I must go, Daisy. I've done nothing at home all weekend with helping Tom and I've got a meal to prepare for this evening."

"Have fun."

"Oh, I will."

"Are you sure your mother won't mind me tagging along?" Thyme said, stretching her scarf nervously across her knees.

"She loves visitors. She always prepares mounds of food."

"Is that where you got your passion for cooking?"

"I guess so ... she loves baking."

"I don't think we should tell her we've been to Scotland together; she might read too much into it."

"I'll tell her you're helping me with the proof reading. That's the truth. Look, I've been thinking. I wondered if you'd like me to do a service for Matt. We could light a few candles, say some prayers; you could read a poem or something. I could make it like a service of thanksgiving for his life." He couldn't see her face but he knew she was crying. "I don't know what you feel about this but you could use it to build bridges ... invite Ben and Bella and Neil and his family."

"I'd really like that."

"We'll always talk about him, Thyme."

She sniffed. "What are you saying?"

"I mean we'll talk about Matt whenever you want."

She was smiling now, he sensed it. "Thank you Jon. This is just the sort of conversation I might have had with your dad ... he was a good friend to me. He was the sort of father I would have liked. Mine was a waste of space. Your dad was a good listener, too. I wish I'd said something to him at the time, it might have helped."

"He was a very patient man, intelligent, spiritual. He liked a joke, that's what I remember about him and his obsession with Dylan Thomas."

"I hope we'll be friends, too."

"I am your friend. I thought you knew that?"

"I thought I was just a lost soul," she said.

"You're much more than that ... do you know Under Milk Wood?"

"I've read it, yes."

"My father loved to recite the prayer of the Rev. Eli Jenkins," he said. "If he was here now, I'm sure he would have quoted this at you ... apologies for the Welsh accent, his was much better ... '*We are not wholly bad or good And Thou I know wilt be the first, To see our best side not our worst'*. We all make mistakes and, hopefully, we learn from them. They don't define us as people unless we let them ... this is it. She's in the ground floor flat."

"I really hope she doesn't mind me gate-crashing your evening."

"It'll be fine," he said. "You're with me."

Diana had dressed in a woollen tunic and tailored trousers, her silvering hair brushed into a shining bob, her eyes expertly kohl-lined. She sighed as she checked the table. That was another down-side to the flat. The kitchen was too small for a table and the breakfast bar barely big enough for two. They were going to have to eat at the drop-leaf table tucked behind the sitting room door.

She glanced at the picture of her husband and then took hold of it, brushing off the wispy veil of dust resting on the frame. She traced the contours of his face, his smiling mouth that was so like Jon's, the firm chin and then she set it back down again. "The boy's coming round," she said. "I'm looking forward to seeing him. I hope he enjoyed the break. He works too hard, just like you did. I still don't know what to do about the vase though ...”

The doorbell rang and she went to pick up the entry-phone in the hall. “Yes ... who is it?”

“Hi Mum, I hope I’m not too late.”

“No, I’ll let you in.” She pressed the buzzer and heard the outside door click open. She went to greet him and then stopped in her tracks when she saw he was not alone.

“I’ve got someone with me,” he said. “This is ...”

“I know who it is, hello Thyme. It’s good to see you. I heard about your accident. How’s the leg?”

“Much better thanks ... I hope you don’t mind me coming uninvited.”

“I invited you,” Jon said. “Thyme’s going to help with the book, proof reading. I didn’t think you’d mind if I brought her with me.”

“I’m pleased you did. Let me take your coats. I’m sorry about your aunt, Thyme. I know you two were close. How are you getting on with everything?”

“We’ve sold the flat.”

“That’s good. Property can be such a headache. You think you have it sorted and then the chain falls through at the last minute. It happened to us several times when we were trying to buy this flat.”

“Yes, we were lucky.”

“Are you staying in Upfordham now? It must seem strange being here again after all this time.”

“I don’t know how long I’ll be here. I still have a few months left on my lease. I suppose it depends on my leg.”

“I hope you’ll be here for the book launch.”

“Maybe,” she said.

“Can I do anything to help?” Jon said.

“It’s all done. Sit down, both of you; I’ll fetch another knife and fork. Is lasagne all right?”

“Suits me,” Jon said.

"I love lasagne."

"That's good. I seem to remember your mum was a vegetarian."

"Yes, but Neil and I liked sausages too much to give up meat ... I think we would have starved without toad in the hole."

"Toad in the hole with a twist is one of the recipes in my book," Jon said.

"I'll have to give it a try ... what's the twist?"

"I bet it's the mustard," Diana said as she returned with the knife and fork.

He laughed. "You'll have to buy the book. So what's been going on while I've been away?"

"There's a bit of sad news I'm afraid," Diana said as she dished up. "Mary Briggs died."

"Oh no ... that was sudden."

"It was a shock for all of us. I've tried to be there for Tom. It was a blessing in a way. He won't have to watch her get any worse."

"Poor Tom ... I intended to call round when I got back. He'll want to discuss the funeral."

"It will be a big one; Mary knew everyone and I think there's family abroad. I do have some good news."

"Go on."

"He's had an offer for the painting."

"That's amazing, how much?"

"The reserve price; I haven't agreed to anything yet. I thought you might want to put it back in the auction, try for more."

"No. I think we should go with the reserve."

"I'll tell him to sort it ... and we've arranged a date for the book launch, the first weekend in May."

"That should just about give us time for all the editing, printing, checking."

"How did you get on over the weekend?"

"Much better than I thought. It only needs another quick session and then I'm done."

"It's really good," Thyme said. "I've had a sneaky peek."

"I'm glad you're helping him. He tries to do too much. Anyone for seconds?" she said, serving spoon poised.

"I've had enough," Jon said.

"So have I, thank you, it was delicious."

"Now, who'd like ice cream?"

"Yes please," Jon said.

Thyme shook her head. "I couldn't."

"Here, let me help you with those," he said as his mother struggled with the pile of empty plates. He followed her into the kitchen.

"How is she?" Diana whispered.

"What do you mean?"

"You know ... the accident."

"That's all it was, Mum, an accident. She's doing ok, just a bit low with her aunt and everything. I'm trying to cheer her up."

"The proof reading should help. It will give her something else to think about."

"That's what I thought."

She bent down to rifle through the freezer. "Do you want raspberry ripple or chocolate?"

"Do you really need to ask?"

She pulled out the tub of chocolate ice cream. "You *will* call Tom, won't you? He's not in a very good place at the moment."

"It will be my first job ... after I've made a fuss of Pandora of course. I hope she's been ok without me."

"Mrs. Ram's been checking on her. I would have kept an eye if you'd asked."

"I know, but it was only a few days. It didn't seem worth

bothering you."

"What else have I got to do these days? Next time, just ask."

"I've had another text," Neil said.

Chantal looked up from her marking and pushed her glasses to the top of her head. "What now?"

"She's back."

"Good. Now you can stop worrying."

"Can I?"

"Go round and see her if it makes you feel better."

"It's too late now. She'll be tired. I'll go tomorrow."

"Now Amy's well enough to go back to school, why don't you call in when you've dropped her off?"

"I could, I suppose."

She tapped her glasses back into place and re-connected with the A4 sheets. "Just do it, Neil. You know you want to and don't forget I'm taking the girls to the dentist after school tomorrow."

"I hadn't forgotten. I might actually get on with some work at last. I'll have a nice long day without any interruptions."

CHAPTER 24

Daisy was in the office when Jon walked over the next morning. "Am I glad you're back," she said.

"I've only been gone four days."

"I know but all hell's broken loose; Thyme Sykes has gone missing, Mary Briggs died and John Meeks has left Rachel."

"Thyme's fine. I've seen her. Mum told me about Mary Briggs. I've spoken to Tom but I didn't know about Rachel. Is she ok?"

"She's quite angry. He's set up home with someone else and it's worse than that ..."

"I hope we're not gossiping here."

"No, it's the truth; she told me he's had children with that woman ... the children she always wanted and he refused to have with *her.*"

"That's harsh. I'd better go and see her."

"She didn't have a clue what had been going on. Now she says she's going to have a party to demolish his wine cellar. Rachel doesn't throw her money about. She doesn't do parties. It's as if she's had a personality change."

"It's probably the shock. I hope she knows what she's doing. Do you think she'd be in now?"

"I don't know. Give her a ring. How did you get on with the book?"

"Very well indeed; another couple of hours should finish it. Thyme's offered to proof read it for me." Daisy's eyes bore into him. "What?" he said.

"I hope *you* know what you're doing."

"It's just a bit of proof-reading ... she was a librarian."

“She is also attractive, in need of tlc and quite vulnerable,” she said watching his colour rise. “She might get the wrong idea.”

“Do you want to proof read the book?”

“I don’t have the time.”

“She needs a friend, Daisy. I’m just extending the hand of friendship, that’s all.”

It was nearly ten o’clock when Neil arrived at Thyme’s house. “I knew it would be you,” she said.

“You look better.” The bruising had faded and he was pleased to note the shadows around her eyes had gone. Her hair was freshly washed; damp waves framed her elfin face. He could hear the washing machine spinning; he could detect the scent of fabric conditioner. She was obviously keeping on top of things. His face relaxed into a smile. “I thought you might need some shopping and anyway I wanted to check everything was ok. Texts don’t tell you much,” he said, elbowing the door shut behind him.

“I don’t need any shopping. How’s Amy?”

“Fighting fit ... she’s back at school now and I can get on with some work at last.”

“I was going to ask you to do something for me ... but if you’re too busy it doesn’t matter.”

“No, it’s fine. What do you want me to do?”

“I’m still not too good on the stairs. I certainly wouldn’t chance the loft ladder. Could you go up in the attic and bring down a suitcase for me?”

“You’ve only just come back ... surely you’re not going away again so soon.”

“There are some things I want to show you. They’re in the case.”

“What’s it like,” he said, heading for the stairs.

“Big, navy blue, you can’t miss it.”

"Is this it?" he called from the top of the loft ladder as he stood astride a mock-leather case that had seen better days.

She hobbled out to see. "Yes. Bring it down."

He slid the case down the ladder and then followed behind. "I don't know how you got this up there on your own," he said as he heaved it into the sitting room and left it on the floor in front of them. "It's a bit heavy." He sank down on the couch next to her. "I hope you're not going to ask me to put it back up there again."

She studied her hands clasped together in her lap. "No ... open it," she said.

He bobbed down onto the carpet next to the case and flipped both catches before pressing the lock. The lid sprung open to reveal something akin to Santa's sack. The case was stuffed with packages wrapped in paper decorated with a variety of patterns, shooting stars, cartoon animals, red foil. He stared up at her. "It's full of presents. What's going on, Thyme?"

"Read the labels," she said.

He chose one at random, wrapped in paper covered in giant footballs. "*To Matt with love from Mum*," he read. He took another, larger one, squashy and striped. "*Happy birthday, Matt ...*" he looked at a third and then a fourth. "Who's Matt?" he said.

She cleared her throat, eyes wide with apprehension. "You're asking the wrong question," she said. "You should be asking, who's 'Mum'."

"You're not ... he's not ..."

"He was my baby."

"Your baby ... oh God, Thyme," he said sinking back onto his heels.

"I had an abortion."

"I'm so sorry. Was Ollie the father?" She nodded.

"What happened?"

"He didn't want to be a father. He didn't want me. He

wanted to live his own life in New Zealand without me. Mum didn't know what to do. Aunt Lal took me up to Scotland and sorted it all out when you were in France but we'd left it so late I had to give birth to the baby."

He let out a distressed sigh. "Why didn't you tell me?"

"It's not the sort of thing you want to tell your kid brother. Anyway, I thought you knew. It wasn't until the other day I realised you didn't ... when you came round on his birthday, of all days with a bottle of fizz. You wanted us to celebrate. I knew then that you hadn't got a clue. Before that I presumed you hadn't said anything because you thought it might upset me, not because you didn't know."

"What's with all the presents?"

"That was Aunt Lal's idea. I bought him one every year on his birthday intending to give them to charity but I couldn't bring myself to do it."

"I knew something was wrong. Chantal thought you had a secret lover."

"She has a wild imagination."

"You were with someone this weekend, though and it wasn't Jill. She was in the shop, I saw her."

"It was Jon Driver."

"Your vicar ..."

His disbelieving tone made her smile. "I've told you ... he's not *my* vicar he's a good friend; I needed to talk and he was prepared to listen. I felt as if I'd go mad if I kept it all in any longer."

"I would have listened."

"I thought you'd be annoyed I hadn't mentioned it before."

"I'm not annoyed ... I'm finding this really difficult ... to know that you've had to carry this around with you for so long."

"It was ok when Aunt Lal was here. We talked about it ... well about him mostly; what he might be like now, what he would have done with his life. When she died, as well as losing her, I felt as if I'd lost him again, too."

"I remember how emotional I was when ours were born. It must have been heart-breaking for you, knowing he couldn't live."

"Jon said he'd do a service for Matt ... a thanksgiving for his life. Will you come?"

"Of course I will."

"And what about Chantal and the girls ... I'd like you all to be there."

"I'll tell Chantal. I'm sure they'd like to support you."

"Jon said I should invite Ben and Bella. I haven't spoken to them for years but he was their grandson."

"You haven't mentioned Ollie."

"I haven't heard from him since he left for New Zealand. As far as I know, he's still there."

"What about these?" he said with a nod towards the suitcase.

"I can't hang on to them forever."

"You could donate them to the children's ward at the hospital; they're always asking for new toys."

"Hmm ... I could ... but they're not all toys."

"Do you want me to deal with it?" She seemed undecided. "I don't mind. I'll have to un-wrap them first, see what they are, I mean sort out what the hospital might be able to use ... maybe you want to do it."

She shook her head. "You do it," she said. She hobbled over to the suitcase and shut the lid with the end of her crutch. "Take them. I'm ready to let them go now. I don't want to see them again."

"Ok. I had something to tell you."

"What ... the flat hasn't fallen through has it?"

"No, nothing like that; I had a call from the solicitor before I came over ... Dad's been in contact."

"What did he want?"

"What does he always want?"

"Oh, I see. Money," she said.

"Spot on. He asked if he'd been mentioned in the will."

"She didn't want him to have any of her money."

"I know. The solicitor thought he'd better warn me he's been sniffing around. He might get in touch."

"He doesn't know where I am."

"He can easily find out. Upfordham's not like London."

"He won't, he wouldn't dare ... would he?"

"Who knows ... will you be all right on your own ... you could come back with me if you like."

"I can't keep hiding out at your house."

"I don't mind."

"No, you want to work. I'm going round to Jill's later. I'll be fine."

CHAPTER 25

All the Committee members were seated in a circle in Daisy's conservatory as if they were about to hold hands and contact the spirit world. Owen leant across to caress the tough fronds of one of her statement plants. "What's this one?" he asked.

"Australian red cordyline," she said. "It should really be in the garden but I haven't had a chance to plant it."

"I've got one up at the allotment," Ben said. "They're indestructible."

"I've always fancied a conservatory," Vi said. "But I don't have the room. I've only got a yard at the back."

"You know you can come round here any time," Daisy said. "Anyway, I thought we'd discuss how far on we were with everything before we have coffee. Who wants to start?"

"Owen asked me about the Punch and Judy," Ben said. "I'm happy to do a show for you."

"That's good. It should encourage the young families to turn up."

"I have the table plan," Owen said. He took a large piece of paper from his file and unfolded it, spreading it out over his knees. "I knew you'd be busy with other things, Daisy. You probably haven't had time to think about tables."

Daisy smiled benignly and produced her own sheet of paper with the tables marked out on a grid. "Let's compare notes later," she said. "We've only got four weeks left now. Has Angela finished her cards?"

"She's made thirty but she won't charge more than two pounds fifty. I don't think that's enough."

"It's all anyone will pay," Rachel said.

"Two pounds fifty is ample," Daisy said. "How are the raffle prizes coming on?"

"We've got ten big ones and some toys so far," Marion said. "I'm still collecting ... the Sunday school have offered to help."

"Have you made your cake?"

"Yes, the cake's ready."

"Well, I'm impressed. Everything seems to be on track."

"Not quite," Vi said.

"What have we forgotten?"

"We still haven't booked someone to open the fair."

"Not a problem," Owen said. "I have a lot of contacts at County Hall. I'm sure I could come up with an ex-mayor ... or someone."

"There's no need," Daisy said. "I already have someone in mind."

"Who's that?" Rachel said.

"I can't tell you yet but I've asked the question and I'm waiting for a response."

"Surely you can tell us," Owen said.

"I'll tell you when I'm sure. You'll just have to trust me."

Owen grunted. "Committees are supposed to work together. We don't just want a local nobody ... we're trying to raise money here. We need a name that will draw in the crowds."

"Daisy knows what she's doing," Rachel said. "I trust her."

"Yes, so do I," Vi said.

"Does the vicar know who it is?" Owen countered, not prepared to be side-lined in such an obvious way.

"He does and he's left me to sort it out."

"That's good enough for me," Rachel said. "Have we finished now?"

"Not quite," Daisy said. "We haven't arranged the publicity. I want you to do that, Owen; posters, adverts in the local press and whatever else you can think of."

"I'll need to know who's opening the fair to do that," he said with a smug look.

"I should be able to tell you next week. Right, *now* we've finished. Over to you, Rachel."

"Thank you Daisy ... well, I'd like to invite you all to drinks at my flat next Sunday after church."

"What are you celebrating ..." Joan asked. "Is it your ruby wedding anniversary?"

"No."

"It's not a significant birthday, is it?" Marion asked.

"It's to celebrate John's retirement," Owen said.

"It's none of those things," Rachel said. "John won't be there. He's left me for someone else and before you say anything, I couldn't be more delighted ... oh yes and I'm donating six bottles of wine to the raffle."

Having suggested the service for Matt, Jon decided he should speak to Ben and Bella about it. He knew it would be hard for Thyme to approach them and he wanted to make it easy for her. A phone call was too impersonal for something so sensitive. He decided to call round. "Now, where's my diary, Pan?" he said. The cat was sitting on the rug in his office, watching. She licked a paw and proceeded to have a quick wash as he checked his availability. "No time like the present," he added "... don't bother to get up ... I'll let you know how I get on."

He could hear the television mumbling away as he waited for someone to answer his knock and then Ben appeared. "Come in, vicar," he said, his forehead scrunching like tissue paper as his eyes lit up. "You missed a good meeting this afternoon."

"Yes, I'm sorry about that. I had to go and see the Bishop."

"Daisy kept us all in order."

"She's great, isn't she? I hope I'm not disturbing you."

"The television you mean ... no, Bella always has that on whether she's watching it or not."

"How is she?"

He shrugged his shoulders. "Much the same," he said. "This Thyme thing is still bothering her."

"That's why I'm here."

Ben opened the sitting room door. "Right," he said and then raised his voice above the babble. "The vicar's here."

Bella was reclining on the sofa. She looked up at him and then flipped the sound down with the remote. Mimi yapped and jumped off her lap to check him over. He tickled her ears. "I expect she's interested in all the cat smells," he said as she continued to sniff at his shoes.

"I didn't know you had a cat," Bella said.

"Oh yes ... Pandora. She's sixteen now."

The hooded lids opened a smidgeon wider. "That's very old for a cat; come and sit down."

"I'll get us some tea," Ben said.

"Not yet, Ben," Jon said. "I want you both to hear what I have to say. Since I saw you last I've had a long chat with Thyme."

Bella snorted and swung her legs off the sofa. "I don't have to listen to this," she said.

"I'd like you to listen," he said.

She hesitated for a moment and then rose to her feet. "No," she said.

Ben stood up beside her and grabbed her arm, at the same time pushing her gently backwards. "Sit down. The vicar's taken the trouble to come round, the least we can do is listen to him."

"Thanks, Ben. I want you to bear in mind that Thyme is in a very vulnerable state at the moment. It's not just her physical injuries, she's upset about her aunt's death ... but there's something else that's been bothering her for years."

"What's that?" Ben asked.

"It's the death of her baby."

"That's sad," Ben said. "It's sad to lose a baby, isn't it Bella?"

Bella stayed silent, staring at the dog curled up like a woollen pompom in her lap.

"It happened a long time ago," Jon said.

"Was she married?" Ben said.

"No."

"What happened to the father?"

"I think you both know that," Jon said.

"No," Ben said. "We don't know. We lost touch with her after Ollie left, didn't we, Bella?"

"It was Ollie's baby," he said.

Ben shook his head. "It can't have been. He's in New Zealand. He would have said ... *she* would have said."

Jon waited for Bella to respond and when she didn't, he prompted an answer. "She did, didn't she, Bella. It was Ollie, wasn't it?"

Her eyes rose slowly to meet Ben's. "I didn't believe her," she said.

"Why didn't you say anything to me?"

"She drove Ollie away. I thought she was telling lies."

"What happened to the baby," Ben said.

"Perhaps Thyme should tell you that," Jon said.

Bella started to shake. "Are you all right?" Ben said.

"She had an abortion, didn't she?" she said, her voice wavering.

"Yes," Jon said.

She howled like an injured animal and then rocked to and fro on the chair, tears streaming from her eyes as Mimi jumped off her lap and went to hide under the coffee table. "See ... see what she's done and you want me to forgive her," she said between sobs and then she got up and surprised them both by running from the room.

Ben stared at Jon, his expression a mixture of disbelief and distress. "It's hard to take in," he said.

"It must be. I'm sorry I upset Bella."

"I'll go after her."

"I hope she's all right."

"She will be."

"There was something else ... but it can wait."

"Right you are vicar," Ben said. He picked up the dog and lumbered towards the door. "Can you see yourself out?"

"Yes of course ... I'll be in touch."

Diana had given herself a good talking to. The vase was hers to sell. She could not believe that such an ugly thing could be so valuable but Tom must know what he was talking about and Jon needed money.

Andrew had liked the vase. Her mother had liked the vase. It was logical to assume that someone else might take a fancy to it as well. She had said nothing to anyone about its prospective sale and so she had nothing to lose if it bombed. It might do well at auction and bring her a nice little windfall.

Her hand reached out for the phone. She hauled it in. What was stopping her? She had every right to sell it but she felt disloyal parting with something that had been in the family for so long. That was silly. It was an object ... a vase ... and not a very pretty one at that. She didn't need it cluttering up the flat. She would sell.

As she tapped Tom's number into the phone she glanced across at Andrew's photo. He would not have stopped her if it meant Jon were to benefit, she was sure of that. Yes, she had his approbation. It felt right. "Could I speak to Tom please?" The relief at finally making a decision was intoxicating. She felt a warm glow as she waited for him to pick up. "Tom, it's Diana, I've made up my mind. I'm going to sell."

CHAPTER 26

Thyme had hobbled round to the newsagents on the way back from Jill's. She felt good, optimistic about the future and in charge of her life. Her aches and pains were getting better every day. Talking about Matt, doing something for him, acknowledging his existence had made a big difference.

She had been delighted and touched when Jon had suggested holding a service for him. Sharing the secret had not diminished Matt as she had feared; on the contrary it had made him more real. She knew the chances of her ever having another child were slim and although there were no photographs and no baby clothes to remember him by, nothing tangible to prove his existence, she would now have the service and the knowledge that others knew, to give her strength.

She was skimming the headlines in the Recorder on her way back home when she became aware of footsteps on the pavement behind her. She slowed down. They slowed down. She tried to move faster and then turned her head briefly hoping to see a fellow shopper, a dog walker, a neighbour heading for home. Her heart sank. She gripped the newspaper, folding her arms tightly across her chest as she realised who he was.

"You look as if you've been in the wars," he said. "I was hoping I might bump into you."

It had been years; years and years since they had last met. Despite the leathery skin and receding hair line, she had no trouble in recognising him. "What are you doing here?" she said breathlessly, trying not to reduce her pace.

"That's a nice way to greet your father."

"Have you seen Neil?"

"I wanted to see you."

"Why now, all of a sudden?"

"We need to talk about Lal."

"I've got nothing to say to you."

"Come on, Thyme."

She had to think fast if she wanted him to leave her alone. She said the first thing that came into her head. "I'm on my way to church."

"Church ... it's not Sunday."

"It's Evensong; I go every day, they're expecting me," she babbled.

"I didn't know you were into religion."

"There's a lot about me you don't know."

"They won't miss you this once. Let's go for a coffee."

"I don't want a coffee." She thought they must look ridiculous carrying on a conversation as they walked along in single file. Gradually she pulled away, hobbling along as fast as her leg would allow.

"Say one for me," he called and then gave up, striding off in the opposite direction.

Neil wasn't home when Chantal returned from the dentist with the girls. "Dad's not here," Amy said.

"We know that ... duh," Alice said as she continued to send and receive messages on her phone. "His car wasn't in the drive."

"Give him a ring ..." Chantal said. "He went to see Thyme but he should have been back by now. He wanted to get on with some writing. I hope she's ok."

"Hi, dad, where are you?" Alice said. "Cool, I'll tell Mum. See you ... he's on his way back from the hospital."

"Oh no ... I wonder what's happened now. You two get changed out of your school clothes."

"Do we have to?" Alice said.

"Yes, you do and then you can think about homework."

"I haven't got any."

"Neither have I," Amy said.

"You can still get changed. Go on ... upstairs."

"Dad's back," Alice called as she charged up the stairs after Amy, forgetting for a minute that she was far too mature to do such a thing.

Chantal waited in the kitchen for Neil. "Is she ok?" she said, searching his face for signs of distress.

"She's fine."

"Alice said you were on your way back from the hospital. Are *you* ok?"

"I'm fine too and I've found out what's been bugging Thyme."

"Have you, I'm glad ... what is it?"

"You're not going to believe this."

"What ... she got married and didn't tell you?"

"You're way out. She had an abortion years ago."

"Thyme was pregnant?"

"It was when she and Ollie were engaged. She thought Mum told me, but she didn't. When he said he didn't want the baby she didn't know what to do. Mum wasn't much help. Aunt Lal helped her sort it out when she decided she couldn't cope but she'd left it so long to make up her mind that she had to give birth to the baby. It was a little boy."

"No ..."

"He was a proper little baby, Charne."

"It must have been heart-wrenching."

"She called him Matthew; she told the vicar and he's doing a service for him."

"Like a sort of memorial service?"

"That's the idea. She'd like us to be there."

"We must be there."

"What about the girls?"

"We'll have to tell them."

"Yes, but how will we explain about the abortion?"

"They don't live in a perfect Enid Blyton world, Neil. I think you'll find they know what's what. Children these days have everything thrust in their faces twenty-four seven. I don't like them watching Corrie and Eastenders but I'm sure they do, if not here, then at their friends' houses. They will feel sorry for her and sad that she felt she had to do it ... but they're not going to judge her."

"Where are they?"

"Upstairs. Call them down we'll do it now."

"Wait a minute ... don't you want to know what I was doing at the hospital?"

"Oh yes, what were you doing?"

"This is the weird bit. She bought a present for Matt every year on his birthday. It was Aunt Lal's idea to make her feel less guilty; she was going to give them to charity ... but she didn't do it."

"She didn't buy the presents."

"No, she bought the presents, but she kept them hidden away in a suitcase; she'd wrapped them up, written labels, everything. She showed me."

"I can't bear it ... I'm going to cry in a minute ... poor Thyme."

"She said she was ready to let them go now so I took the toys up to the children's ward at the hospital ... I brought the rest of it back with me. I'll take it to the charity shop with Aunt Lal's stuff."

"That must have been so emotional for her. You haven't left her on her own."

"She'd been invited round to Jill's for tea. She was much happier when I left. I think she'll be ok now."

"And we never knew ... she was trying to deal with all this

on her own."

"Aunt Lal was there for her, but when she died, it all came to a head; she needed to talk to someone. That's where the vicar comes into it. He listened and suggested the service. She wanted Matt to be acknowledged as a person. He existed and all this time she's had to pretend he didn't ... it's unbelievable."

"This Ollie doesn't sound very nice."

"I didn't have much to do with him. He was a few years older than me."

"What a waste of a life," she said. "All those years grieving, feeling guilty, not able to make another relationship; I feel really bad. I should have talked to her more. I never have time for anything."

"A waste of two lives," he said, "What about poor little Matt?"

"Don't," she said. "Just don't."

"That's not all ... my father has been hanging around; he's been to see the solicitor to find out if there's anything for him in Aunt Lal's estate."

"You've seen him?"

"No but as soon as Mr. Phillips from the solicitors rang to let me know, I realised Amy has. She said she saw a strange man outside the house the other day. They must have given him our address. They know I'm dealing with everything. I'm glad he didn't knock on the door. I don't know what I'd have said to him."

"Has Thyme seen him?"

"I'm sure she hasn't. She would have said."

"She doesn't need any more stress."

"I warned her he was over here."

"Perhaps you'd better check."

CHAPTER 27

Diana was just about to leave the house when Daisy called the next day. “Have you got a minute?” she said.

“I was only going to call in on Tom, it can wait; he wants me to help planning the funeral; he’s got an old family friend coming over from South America ... well, the son of an old family friend. I think she’s too frail to attend.”

“You’ve done a few.”

“I’ve lost count how many. I can certainly help with choosing the music and I can show him Andrew’s book of appropriate readings. What can I do for you?”

“I wanted to know if you’d heard about Thyme’s service.”

“No ...”

“I thought Jon may have mentioned it.”

“I haven’t seen him since he came round for a meal with her after his weekend away.”

“That’s interesting.”

“Daisy will you stop being mysterious. Just tell me what’s going on.”

“To be honest, I don’t know. Jon seems different since his weekend away. I wondered if he’d said anything to you.”

“He seemed fine to me. He doesn’t give much away. He doesn’t want his mother interfering; he’s always been like that.”

“I’m wondering if there’s something going on with him and Thyme.”

Diana laughed. “I’d be the last person to find out if there was but I very much doubt it. I think he’s trying to boost her confidence. He asked her to do some proof reading for him. He sees her as a vulnerable person in need of tlc, that's all."

"I've also noticed that you seem to be spending a lot of time with Tom."

"I hope you're not going to suggest that we're an item?"

"You could do worse."

"I'm twice his age."

"If you were a man and he was a woman no-one would think it was wrong; did anyone try to stop you from marrying Andrew?"

"No, but ..."

"And Tom is very attractive ... and available."

"Well, we're just good friends."

"You've got that 'I know something you don't know', look Diana ... just like when you found out about Judy Hobbs and the geography teacher."

Diana laughed. "For heaven's sake, Daisy, it's nothing like that ...but you're right, there is something ..."

"Tell me."

"No, I can't; not yet. I don't want to tempt fate. You'll just have to be patient."

The cat was stretched out on Jon's bed. He stroked her back. "I'm going to visit Thyme," he said. She mewed plaintively. "No, don't tell me I should leave it. The book's ready for proof reading and I've pencilled in a date for Matt's service; I have to talk to her about that so I might as well do it now." She raised her head and stared at him with inscrutable eyes. "Don't look at me like that. I'm not going to change my mind. I know, I know, I've already got several other calls to make but I should just be able to fit it all in."

The lent groups were taking up a lot of his time and the extra services he had laid on had shrunk his available slots even further. Pastoral visits had suffered. It was after eight o'clock when he finally made it to Thyme's house. He parked the bike and removed the manuscript from one of the panniers attached either side of the seat.

He knew something was wrong the minute he saw her. The haunted look was back, the shadows under her eyes, the nervous sleeve-tweaking. "I came to leave the manuscript with you," he said. "And I've got a date for Matt's service."

"I'm sorry ... can we do this some other time, I don't feel up to it this evening."

"Of course, we can re-schedule. Are you all right?"

"Not really ... my father has just had a go at me on the phone."

"Anything I can do to help?"

She shook her head. "We haven't been in touch for years and then I bumped into him at the shops the other day. I told him I had nothing to say to him but he got my phone number from somewhere. He's up to his old tricks. It all boils down to money. I'm waiting for Neil to call round. He should be here in a minute. I thought you were him."

He turned towards the road. "I think I heard a car."

"Yes, here he is ... this is Fr. Jon, Neil."

Jon held out a friendly hand. "How are you?"

"Good thanks," Neil said.

"Well, I'd better crack on ... bye, Thyme. You know where I am if you need me."

She hobbled back inside and Neil shut the door behind them leaving him outside in the cold. He re-filled the pannier and wheeled the bike out into the road, surprised at how rejected he felt. He wanted to be in the house with them. He wanted to be her champion, to fight her corner, protect her from the world and all its troubles. He wondered how much longer he could keep his feelings to himself. It was ironic that Daisy suspected something might be going on between them. He had tried hard not to let it show.

He understood a little of how Thyme must have felt,

keeping Matt quiet. He had an overwhelming desire to tell her how he felt but he couldn't. How could he? His role seemed to be that of confidante, father confessor, counsellor. Sadly she had shown no signs of seeing him in a more romantic role.

Daisy had recommended an uncomplicated wife. He didn't care how complicated she was or how much of a muddle her life had become. It was Thyme he wanted and no-one else.

"This is all we need," Chantal said, "Your father causing trouble. We'll need to keep an eye on Thyme as well as the children."

"I hope she doesn't crack and give him some of Aunt Lal's cash."

"There's no reason why she should. The will was quite clear."

"There weren't likely to be any loopholes with her being a solicitor."

"Exactly ... he's just trying it on," she said.

"Thyme's a soft touch, especially at the moment. The vicar was round there when I called."

"What did he want?"

"I don't know. She didn't say."

"I'm glad you brought her back with you. She'll be safe here. At least your father won't be able to call on her at home. It's bad enough that he had a go at her on the phone. How did he get her number?"

"I don't know ... he might have asked Jill. He was always good at sweet-talking the ladies. I'll ring the solicitor in the morning ... arrange a meeting with him in his office. We don't want him coming round here. He can just slope off back to Spain. Thyme doesn't need to get involved."

"You're not planning to give him some of the proceeds from the flat are you?"

"No I am not. I want him to see he can't mess with us. He

chose to leave when he did. He didn’t help mum when she was struggling. We don’t owe him a thing and apart from that, Aunt Lal didn’t want him to have any of her money.”

CHAPTER 28

The bowls of fruit and vases of flowers lent a festive air to the tastefully decorated flat. Knots of people were chatting as Rachel emptied bottles like a boatswain baling a boat, buzzing between her guests with wasp-like enthusiasm.

Ben and Bella were seated on one of the leather sofas placed at right-angles to the living flame fire opposite Joan and Fred who had just sat down on the other one. Fred took a long draft of beer from a pewter tankard.

"It's a shame you don't drink wine," Ben said. "This is good stuff."

"You can't beat a Hopping Hare," Fred said as he wiped froth from his mouth with the back of his hand.

"We brought it with us," Joan said exchanging a meaningful glance with Bella. "Rachel said there was only wine on offer."

"She seems keen to get rid of it."

"I wonder if John knows what she's doing," Fred said.

"I don't think she cares," Ben said.

"Why should she?" Bella said. "What he did was dreadful."

Joan nodded. "Dreadful," she echoed.

Owen had managed to corner Daisy behind one of the sofas. "I've had the posters made," he said as he sipped a glass of John's Viognier. "I pinned one to the church notice-board. The library's taken a couple and Georgia's got some in her car. She drives all over the place with her mobile hair-dressing business. I've brought the rest with me for the others to distribute."

"Good. I saw the advert in the Recorder."

"Yes, it came out quite well."

"It was bigger than I imagined it would be."

"I thought we should invest in half a page. We needed something eye-catching with only a week to go."

"Can I butt in," Diana said. "I wanted to say that I thought Isobel Flynn was an inspired choice to open the fete."

"I thought it was appropriate with one of her paintings making a decent contribution to the fund ..."

"... and her local connections," Diana said.

"She seemed keen to do it."

"I can't wait to meet her."

"I don't know what was wrong with asking the mayor," Owen said.

"Has everyone got enough to drink?" Rachel said her cheeks flushed with triumph. "There's plenty here. Owen ... let me top you up."

He looked across to Angela, deep in conversation with Bella. Ben had lumbered off to get a refill. "Who's driving home, Ange?" he barked.

"You are. I've already had two."

He sighed. "It looks like I've had my quota," he said. "It's a shame, that's good wine. Whatever else you might say about him, John knows his stuff where wine's concerned."

"Here," Rachel said handing him an unopened bottle. "Take some home with you. I want everybody to take a bottle home with them. Where's the vicar?"

"He had to go and see someone," Daisy said.

"Take him two bottles," Rachel said.

"We're off now," Owen said. "Do you want me to take them?"

Daisy smiled at him sweetly. "I can manage thanks. I'll see you on Friday night."

"Friday night?"

"We always set up the tables for the fair on a Friday night," Vi said. "It's too much of a rush in the morning."

"Right, ladies, I'll see you all on Friday night. What time,

Daisy?"

"Seven o'clock," she said.

"Seven o'clock ... did everyone hear that?" he said, raising his voice above the hubbub in the room, "Everyone to the hall at seven o'clock on Friday."

"Can my booth wait until Saturday morning?" Ben said. "I've got a darts match Friday night. It won't take long."

"That's fine," Daisy said. "You know where we've put you?"

"Owen showed me ... on the stage."

"We thought it would give everyone the best view," Owen said. "And don't bring the raffle prizes until Saturday morning. We don't want them to disappear over-night ... have you checked the tea-bags Rachel, we can't risk running out of tea. What about the scones ..."

"Come on Owen," Angela said as she grabbed his arm. "Our dinner will be toast if we don't get back soon ... great party, Rachel. Thanks for having us."

"Can we go to the fair on Saturday, Mum? There'll be a Punch and Judy show," Amy said.

"I used to love Punch and Judies when I was little," Thyme said. "Do you remember the Punch and Judy man at Bournemouth, Neil?" She was sitting on the sofa with her leg resting on the coffee table.

"I think we should all go," he said. "We could do with a bit of fun."

"Do we have to?" Alice said. "I'd rather go and see Sophie."

"She might like to come too," Neil said. "Ask her."

Alice scowled at him. "I don't *think* so," she said.

"You don't have to come if you don't want to," Chantal said.

"I'm going to leave you to it," Thyme said. "Now you've sorted out Dad, there's no reason why I shouldn't be at home."

"Stay for lunch," Neil said. "I'll take you back this afternoon."

She swung her leg off the table and hobbled towards the door. "Ok. I'll go and pack my bag. I'll be glad to get this thing off my leg. It's a real nuisance now I'm feeling better."

"When do I give you a lift to the hospital?"

"Next week," she said.

"Wait a minute ... didn't you want to go up to Scotland?" Chantal said.

"Yes," Amy said. "We were going to see the Kelpies."

Thyme smiled. "So we were."

"Scotland?" Alice said.

"I don't suppose you want to do that, either," Neil said.

"I don't mind. Sophie's been. She said Ben Nevis is awesome."

"That's just as well," Chantal said. "We've already made the booking; we're going ... all of us. It will be good to spend quality time together as a family. I'm thinking of banning mobiles."

"Does that mean grown-ups as well?" Alice said.

"Of course ... no special cases," she said.

"Where are we staying?" Amy said. "Can we take board games?"

Alice groaned. "No phones ... board games ... this is going to be sooo boring."

"It sounds like bliss to me," Thyme said. "It will be an adventure, Alice. I know you'll just love it."

Diana was one of the last to leave the party. She let herself into the flat and gazed about her. It was hard not to make a comparison with Rachel's. Hers was smaller, more cluttered. It was nowhere near as attractive, despite her best efforts. Daisy thought it felt homely. It didn't feel like home to her. It was too small. Goldilocks-style she considered the other homes she knew well; Tom's house was too large, the vicarage too old. Daisy's was just the right size, neither too old nor too new. She lived in a leafy cul-de-sac in a convenient spot. The house had parquet flooring in the hall, the original tiled fireplaces and a beautiful garden. She missed her garden. It was just the sort of house she would have chosen for herself.

She wished they had not moved in such a hurry. Andrew had needed to see her settled; he had needed to be settled. She hoped that one day she would open the door and be glad to be there. That day was a long time coming. She felt restless. Spring was only round the corner. It was a bright afternoon; there was no way she was staying home, alone. She put her coat back on, turned tail and went out again.

Having decided that a brisk walk was what was needed she drove into the village and parked in Cooper's Close. She lingered in the road outside Daisy's house. She contemplated calling on her and then decided against it. They had only just said their goodbyes at Rachel's. She did not want to wear out her welcome. She sauntered slowly past Maggie Watt's house with the 'Sold subject to contract' sign leaning against the fence with a drunken list. She could see bulbs peeping through matted vegetation and an apple tree in need of hard pruning.

The small detached had a symmetrical frontage. Green paint was peeling from the front door and she guessed it would be equally drab inside; Daisy had said Maggie had lost interest in keeping the house up-to-date. The glass panels at the top of the door glinted with promise in the afternoon sun, almost as if the house was winking at her, willing her to take a look, give it a chance. The house would be someone else's project but there were bound to be others, all she had to do was Google 'estate agents'.

She walked on, asking herself if she would prefer a house to the flat. She needed to look into all the extra costs, see if her pension would be enough. Now she was getting ahead of herself. She wouldn't be doing anything unless the vase came up trumps. She thought she might run the idea past Jon to see if he thought it would be a good idea in principle. She hadn't seen him for days. He might enjoy the company. Perhaps she could persuade him to join her for a walk.

The vicarage gardens lacked interest. They had been designed with low-maintenance in mind. It would be a while before the flowering shrubs were at their best. The small patch of grass was worn at the edges where people had taken short-cuts to the front door; no-one had bothered to dead-head the hydrangeas. His motor-bike stood on the path beside his clapped out mini, a sure sign that he was at home. She rang the bell.

"Mum." His sleeves were rolled up to the elbows but he was still wearing his dark trousers and dog collar. "This is a nice surprise."

"It was such a lovely afternoon I decided to go for a walk. I haven't seen you for ages. I thought you might like to join me. There's something I wanted to discuss with you."

"Oh ... sorry ... I'm a bit tied up this afternoon. Is it important?"

"No, no, it's not urgent. It can wait."

"I was trying to get ahead, prepare my sermon for next Sunday. With a busy week coming up and then the fair on Saturday, I wasn't sure when else I'd have the time."

She masked her disappointment with a cheerful smile. "Never mind, it was just a spur of the moment thing. You get on with your sermon."

"I might have time to call in later."

"Don't worry about it. I'll probably see you at the fair if you don't."

She walked on to the duck pond. There were no ducks in evidence; no moorhens dabbling in the rushes. What soil was left on the weedy bank had been flattened into concrete-like mud by people feeding the birds with yesterday's sandwiches. The weeping birches were beginning to produce leaves, small, tender, spiralling down the branches like droplets of water in a waterfall. She was just about to head for home when she saw Tom sitting on a bench a few metres away, staring into the murky water. "Hello," she called.

He looked up at the sound of her voice. His expression lifted. He returned her smile. "Diana ... fancy meeting you here."

"Where have all the ducks gone?"

"I was just wondering the same thing."

"Do you fancy a stroll round the park?"

"I could do with a walk," he said. "And then you can come back to my house for a cup of tea."

"That would be good. What were you doing, sitting there all on your own?"

"I was thinking dismal thoughts."

"We can't have that," she said, tugging him to his feet. "Best foot forward."

He laughed. "Very Mary Poppins ... where's your brolly?"

"It's not going to rain. Look at that gorgeous sky," she said.

He looked up, shielding his eyes from the sun. "Gorgeous," he repeated. "Thanks, Diana."

"What are you thanking me for now?"

"For being my guardian angel ... just when I'm in dire need of a kick in the pants, there you are, chivvying me along."

"I enjoy your company," she said.

"The feeling's mutual."

"I'm glad. It's no fun being lonely."

"Surely you're not lonely," he said. "You always seem so up-beat."

"I meant you but, yes, sometimes I get lonely, too."

He squeezed the gloved hand she had tucked into the crook of his arm. "Have you thought what you're going to do with the money from the vase?"

"I never count my chickens before they're hatched," she said primly.

"I'm sure it's going to make the money tomorrow. If you want some investment advice we can help. Dave's very hot on that side of things. You could start a property portfolio."

"What are you talking about ... at my age?"

"You've got years, yet."

"I hope so. I don't know. I don't want to tempt fate but ... if the vase makes a colossal amount of money I might invest in property."

"You can't go wrong with bricks and mortar. Come and have a word with Dave. He'll set you on the right track."

"I'm not prepared to do anything until after the auction."

"Don't worry, it's a dead cert."

"You said that about my picture."

"It sold in the end, didn't it?"

"Yes, but ..."

"Are you coming to the auction?"

"Definitely not," she said with feeling. "I can't go through all that again. You'll have to let me know when it's over."

CHAPTER 29

Daisy was in the parish office the next morning, going through the accounts when Jon joined her. “Are we solvent?” he said.

“Surprisingly, we are,” she said. “And what’s even better is that I predict after we take into account the sales of your book, your mother’s painting and the takings from the fair, we should have nearly reached the ten thousand pound mark.”

“I hope you’re not being too optimistic. If it rains on Saturday the fair could be a wash-out.”

“I’m checking the weather forecast daily. Countryfile wasn’t predicting a deluge. Can’t you have a word with your Boss?”

“I have, don’t you worry. I’m sure the sun will be cracking the flags,” he said. “Is everyone ready?”

“Ready and raring to go ... we’re good at organising fairs in this parish, even though I do say so myself.”

“I love it when a plan comes together,” he said.

“Has Thyme done the proof reading yet?”

“No. She’s had a few family issues.”

“There have always been issues in that family.”

“Tut tut, Daisy ... judge not lest ye be judged,” he said.

“Don’t say I didn’t warn you.”

“People have been warning me all my life,” he said. “It never does much good.”

“Fair enough,” she said. “Oh ... I nearly forgot. I’ve got something for you.” She reached under the desk to retrieve a supermarket bag. “Here you are ... a gift from Rachel.”

“Wine,” he said. “Is this from John’s stash?”

“She was just giving it away. He’ll be madder than a box of

frogs when he finds out, but by then it will be too late. It serves him right."

"Now, now, Daisy, what have I just told you?"

"I'm not being judgmental," she said. "All I'm saying is that he's made his bed and now he has to lie on it."

Diana woke up feeling like a teenager about to sit an exam. Her stomach was churning. She couldn't settle to anything. Her toast went in the bin. She decided to go for a stroll around Linchester to try and take her mind off the sale. By twelve o'clock she had meandered in and out of practically every shop in the town. She had been planning to have her lunch in the cathedral tea-rooms but she wasn't hungry and she felt exhausted with all the anxiety and anticipation. In the end she went straight home instead.

The flat seemed unnaturally quiet after the buzz of town. Now would have been an ideal time for pottering in the garden, if there had been a garden in which to potter. The feel of soft earth as she prepared a bed for planting, the scent of fresh foliage; the snap of the secateurs bringing order to chaos ... but there were no pots to empty, no plans to be made and Monty Don in wellies didn't quite do it for her. She prepared a sandwich and settled down in front of the television to watch the news; before she knew it she had nodded off. It was a deep, dreamless sleep ultimately disturbed by a persistent ringing.

It took her a few minutes to realise it was the phone and not the front door. Her heart was beating so fast she could barely speak. "Hello," she whispered breathlessly.

"Diana, is that you?"

She cleared her throat and tried to feel more relaxed. "Yes."

"It doesn't sound like you. It's Tom."

"I know it is. What happened with the vase ... is it sold?"

"Yes and you're not going to believe how much money it made. I can hardly believe it myself."

"*Tom* ..." she said menacingly.

He laughed. "All right, it sold for a hundred and eighty thousand pounds."

She gasped and sank to her knees on the floor. "A hundred and eighty thousand ..." she croaked.

"I told you it would."

"I can't believe it."

"I knew you'd be surprised."

"I'm shocked ... it was so ugly."

"Apparently it was quite rare ... and beautiful, if you ask me, we've raked in a substantial amount of commission."

"You didn't tell anyone it was mine, did you?"

"I'm the only one who knows the identity of the seller."

"Who bought it?"

"It was a phone bid from China."

"You were right, then."

"Yes ... if only I could find a few more like it ... I'd be able to retire."

"That's almost the price of a house," she said.

"Several if you're buying up north ... now you can make a start on your property empire."

"I don't want an empire," she said. "I'd be happy with one small detached."

Ben was worried. For the second time that week Bella had refused pudding. He wouldn't have minded but it was her favourite, sticky toffee with home-made custard. He couldn't put it off a moment longer; he would have it out with her at once. Lumbering into the sitting room, he removed the remote from her grip and turned the television off as he took his familiar seat in the armchair opposite. "What is it, old girl?"

"Nothing," she said sulkily. "Why did you do that?"

"You're not getting this back until you tell me what's up," he said. "You didn't eat your pudding ... again ... that's not like you."

"I need to lose weight," she said.

"That's a load of bull," he said. "You've never bothered to diet for as long as I've known you ... what makes you want to do it now?"

"I don't know. It seemed like a good idea. It's been on the news ... all about carrying too much weight. It makes you at risk of diabetes, heart disease ... everything," she finished lamely.

"Right ... well, we'll have porridge for breakfast in future and I'll order carrots instead of crisps this week," he said crossing his legs with grim determination.

She sighed. "I knew about the baby," she said in a small voice.

"I know ... you said."

"She asked for my help."

"Oh, I see."

"I read the letters before I threw them away. I could have stopped her."

"Oh heck ... Bella, Bella, Bella ..." he said, shaking his head.

"She said Ollie didn't want the baby ... why wouldn't he have wanted the baby if it was his child, his own flesh and blood? That's why I didn't believe her. I didn't want to believe her and I didn't want to tell you. It was all my fault Ben ... I could have saved that baby if I'd listened and now I feel like an executioner."

"No," he said. "No, no. If anyone's to blame it has to be Ollie."

"I rang him while you were at the Bandy."

"You never did ..."

"I did. I had to know. He said that she was telling the truth. I feel so stupid ... no guilty. How can I ever hold my head up again?" Two large tears made slow progress down to her wobbling chin.

"You mustn't think like that. Thyme rang me ..."

"You've spoken to her? You didn't say."

"No, well, I was waiting for you to come round. Fr. Jon's arranging a service for little Matt. He said we can't bring him back but we can do something for him ..."

"That's a lovely idea."

"... and it will help Thyme with her feelings of loss. She can't forgive herself for the abortion, you know. She's ashamed of what she's done. She's upset no-one in the family knew about him apart from her mother and her aunt ..."

"And me."

"And you and Ollie of course. She doesn't care what people will say now and neither should you. She wants them to know she had a son if only for a short time. It's going to be a service of thanksgiving for the baby's life. She said we're invited."

"I've always wanted grandchildren," Bella said.

"Shall we go?"

She hesitated. "I'd like to, but ... oh ... I don't know."

"No buts, old girl ... let's do it."

CHAPTER 30

The heavens opened as Diana sat in her car waiting for the estate agent to arrive. She had only contacted Linkmans on the off-chance that they might have a suitable property in her price range. She couldn't believe her luck when she was told Maggie Watts' house had come back on the market. She wound up the window to avoid raindrops spitting through the gap and read the details one more time; *tired* decorations, *compact* kitchen, *manageable* gardens and bathroom in need of *up-dating*. It all sounded like hard work. Would she be taking on too much? She was startled by a brisk tapping on the window. "Good afternoon ... Mrs. Driver?"

He was large with a jovial attitude and a mop of caramel curls. "That's right," she said. She got out and he moved aside to let her pass, holding up an umbrella to protect her from the rain.

"Jack Tighe, Linkmans. I see you have the details with you."

"I was just reading them. It sounds like there's a lot of work to do."

"The whole house is in need of up-dating but most of it is just cosmetic. The condition is reflected in the price ... it's a good buy ... we've had a great deal of interest."

"They told me that when I telephoned your office."

"It's only recently come back on the market."

"Yes ... they said there was some problem with the buyer's mortgage."

"Mortgages are tricky these days."

"Fortunately, this will be a cash purchase."

“I understand you have a flat to sell.”

“I have but it’s not part of this deal.”

“We’d be happy to handle it for you ... this is the lounge,” he said opening the door on a small sitting room almost as cluttered as her flat. He negotiated his way through piles of books and magazines to pull back the rose-swathed curtains. Light flooded into the room highlighting the yellowing wallpaper and dusty ornaments. “The trick is to try and see it without furniture.”

She tried to imagine freshly emulsioned walls either side of the wooden fire surround. She conjured up oak floorboards and her easy chairs. “Yes ... I like the open fire,” she said, her enthusiasm growing.

“You’ll love the morning room,” he said leading the way through to the back of the house.

She took in the tiled fireplace, her glance gliding over to the window seat set below the conventional casement and then the French doors leading through to a small courtyard garden. Even in the rain-washed light it looked cosy. She imagined the evening sun slanting across the room. “I do.” She walked over to the window. “Can we have a look outside? I think the rain’s gone off now.”

“We’ll have to use the back door. I’m afraid I don’t have those keys.”

The kitchen was a square room which she guessed had last been fitted out in the sixties. There was a mug tree on a shelf near the stainless steel sink, four mugs suspended from it in a precarious fashion. The white enamel of the flour bin was chipped and worn; the printed *Flour* label had turned from black to grey. Newspapers littered the Fablon-coated table along with a bowl of over-ripe fruit. She found herself imagining cloud grey walls; generous work-tops sheltering glossy white cupboards and the cracked linoleum replaced with Italian tiles.

He undid the bolts to let in the watery sun, along with a fresh gust of wind. "The paving's still in good order," he said.

She had noticed bulbs piercing the soil in flower beds tucked up against the garden walls; the ivy camouflaging worn mortar and chipped bricks; a stone bird bath which she hoped would be left behind. She didn't want to appear too enthusiastic and lose bargaining power but her heart was hammering in her chest she loved it so much.

"Shall we go upstairs?"

As she followed him up the dark staircase lined with family photographs, she realised that she didn't need to see any more of the house. It was quite obviously a home. She wanted to make it hers.

CHAPTER 31

Pandora was sunning herself on the front doorstep when Jon got back from the supermarket on Friday afternoon. "Time to go inside," he said. "It's getting cold out here." She arched her back and sauntered into the house after him. He checked the phone messages. There was nothing from Thyme. "She still hasn't called," he said. "Right ... I've given her long enough. It's time to be pro-active. Food and then we'll discuss tactics."

His heart was pounding as he trod up the path to her front door a couple of hours later. The light went on almost immediately and he prepared a friendly smile. "Here I am again, the bad penny," he said. She smiled back. He was pleased the shadow of anxiety had left her eyes, he hoped, for good.

"Come in. I'm sorry about last time," she said.

"I've brought the manuscript ... again. Do you still want to do it?"

"Of course I do. I'm looking forward to reading it."

"I've brought you a bottle of wine, as a thank you," he said presenting her with one of the bottles Daisy had given him.

"Thanks. Would you like a glass?"

"I think I would ... this is my last visit of the evening."

"Your *last* visit ... I thought Friday was supposed to be your day off."

"It is, but the world doesn't stop because I'm supposed to have a day off."

"Well, it's kind of you to call on me," she said handing him a glass.

"I look on you more as a friend."

"Oh."

He thought she looked embarrassed and decided he had over-stepped the mark. "I can't stay long. It's another early start in the morning," he went on quickly." I think Daisy expects to see me in the hall when everyone arrives. Did you sort your father out?"

"Neil did. He's been a rock these last few weeks ... well, they all have. I would have been lost without them."

He felt a momentary spark of envy. He doused it at once but could not help feeling he should have been there for her, to protect and comfort; the strength of his reaction shocked him. "Are you ready to talk about Matt's service now?"

"I've been thinking about it a lot ... and about you."

"About me?" he said, his hopes rising.

"I know I can trust you. You've kept my secret. I know you haven't said a word to anyone else ... except to Ben and Bella and I appreciate that."

"I had to say something to Daisy about the service. I'll need help with the candles."

"It's not a secret now."

"I'll do my best to make it meaningful for you."

"I don't know how to thank you, Jon ... you've been so understanding ... it will mean the world to me, a real acknowledgment of his life. I'll feel as if I've done right by him at last but I'm never going to feel good about it."

"I know."

"I couldn't have done anything else at the time ... I thought it was the right thing until it happened. This will be my way of owning up, saying sorry ... I've found something I'd like to read."

"Good. I was going to suggest six o'clock the Friday before Good Friday."

"That should be fine. We're going up to Scotland for a few days the week after. I promised to take Amy to see the Kelpies.

She's horse-mad. They'll all be coming to the service and Ben and Bella. I spoke to Ben on the phone, by the way. He was so sweet about everything. All the family will be there ..."

"You mean all the family except your father and Ollie."

"I've never known what a father is. He left when I was small. I survived. He didn't know about Matt and even if he had, he wouldn't have wanted to help me. All he cares about, has ever cared about, is money. He was over here trying to get us to part with Aunt Lal's cash. Neil said the solicitor put him straight. As for Ollie, he didn't want Matt in the first place."

"I wanted to be sure you had thought it all through. Are you coming to the fair?"

"Yes. I'm looking forward to Ben's Punch and Judy."

"It's something a bit different."

"I would have offered to help if it wasn't for my leg."

"I'm sure Daisy would be glad of an extra pair of hands if you're serious. Shall I ask her?"

"I could collect money at the door or fold some raffle tickets, I suppose."

"I'll get her to call you."

"I am grateful for everything you've done for me," she said. "I hope you know that."

He wanted more but he knew that was out of the question. Would she ever know or understand his feelings for her? "I don't need you to be grateful," he said. "For you to be more at peace with yourself is enough." He stood up. "I'd better be off."

She hobbled over to his side and his heart raced as she reached up to kiss his cheek. "Thanks, anyway," she said. "You're a good friend."

Pandora was there to greet him when he returned to the vicarage. She miaowed loudly and stalked down the drive to meet him. "Well, one step forward and two steps back," he said. "Thanks for asking. Is it ever going to be the right time to tell her how I feel?" He lent down to stroke the cat's ears as she wrapped herself round his leg like pasta round a spoon. "Are you coming in?" Her purring became more leonine than run-of-the-mill moggy. "I'll take that as a yes. Come on then," he said picking her up and carrying her into the house. "Tomorrow is another day."

CHAPTER 32

"Have you got time to come over this evening?"

Diana had visited Tom Briggs so many times over the previous few weeks that she reckoned she could have driven there blind-fold. She was fond of him in the way that an aunt might be fond of a favourite nephew. He needed her support; someone to lean on and she was more than happy to fulfil that role for him. She looked at the photographs spread out over the floor and made a snap decision. She could sift through them another day. "I could be with you in about half an hour."

"Good."

"What's bothering you?"

"I'll tell you when you get here."

She parked the car and crunched up the drive on foot eager to tell him of her visit to Cooper's Close. He must have been watching out for her. As she stretched out her arm to press the bell, the door opened in front of her. "You sounded worried on the phone," she said. "I thought we'd ironed out all the problems."

"It's not about the funeral ... well it is and it isn't. Come into the study. The children are in the sitting room."

"You'll never guess what I've done."

"What have you done?"

"I've been to see a house. I'm thinking of putting in an offer."

"Really ..."

"It's in Cooper's Close," she said, slipping off her coat and tugging her scarf free. She carried them over her arm as she followed him through to the back of the house. "It's already been sold once. It fell through. Daisy said they go quickly down there so I'll have to be quick if I don't want to miss it. It's only got two bedrooms but it's perfect for me."

"Oh." He seemed distant, almost disinterested; depressed?

"Do you think I should put in an offer?"

"If you think it's right for you."

"My sister's asked me to go on a painting holiday with her and when I come back I'll get stuck into the house ... if my offer's accepted. The house hasn't been touched for years. I want to try and do most of the work myself. It'll be a challenge. I couldn't do a lot in the rectory and the flat was already decorated when we moved in, not much scope for change but I've always made my own curtains."

"Right."

His attitude was beginning to worry her. She had thought he had been handling everything reasonably well so far but maybe not. "I'll put the flat on the market. I've asked Linkmans to deal with that for me. I hope you don't mind; it seemed best as they're handling the house sale. They're coming to have a look next week. We've had a chat about it. They don't reckon I'll have a problem."

"It sounds as if you've already made up your mind."

"I have and I haven't; it's a big decision."

"What does Jon think about your plans?"

"I haven't told him yet. I'm hoping to catch up with him at the fair; will you be there?"

"The fair ... no, it's not my thing."

"What's wrong, Tom?"

He shut the door and sat down beside her on the sofa-bed. "I've had an email from Philip Perez."

"Philip Perez?"

"Yes. Carolina was an old friend of Mum's."

"I know ... who is Philip Perez ... her brother?"

"Her son; he's coming over for the funeral as her

representative."

"That's good of him."

"He's only just found out who his father was. She told him he'd died before he was born ..."

"And he hadn't."

"No."

"I'm sorry but I don't understand why this should worry you or concern me."

"His full name is Philip Andrew Perez."

The colour drained from her cheeks. "Andrew was the father ... *my* Andrew?" He nodded silently and her usually composed features fell into disarray. "No, it can't be him."

"I didn't believe it to begin with, but I couldn't think of a logical reason why she should lie about it."

"What's Jon going to say?"

"Did he know about South America?"

"In a roundabout sort of a way; it didn't seem relevant to us as a family."

"It's sort of relevant now."

"Yes."

"How do you think he'll take it?"

"I really don't know. It's such a bolt from the blue."

"How do you feel about it?"

"Shocked ... sad that Andrew never met his son; sad that his son will never meet him."

"He could still meet his half-brother."

"How long will he be staying for?"

"Only overnight; he's doing London before he comes here for the funeral and then flying straight back afterwards."

"Are you absolutely sure about this?"

"As sure as I can be ... why would she make it up after all this time? He didn't know I knew you. I haven't told him yet. I said I knew Andrew and that he'd died but I didn't mention you or Jon. He's keen to track down any relatives he might have over here. I said Sussex was a big county but it wouldn't take much for him to track Jon down."

"You're right. I'd better tell him sooner rather than later. Why didn't Carolina tell Andrew she was pregnant?"

"I don't know. The family has money ... she wouldn't have needed his help to bring up her son. She never married. Philip's an only child. He didn't know much about his father until she decided to tell him everything recently. With Mum dying and her having a heart attack I suppose she thought she should tell him the truth before it was too late."

"And Mary knew nothing about him either?"

"No. She never went out to South America. The families weren't close. Christmas cards every year and that was about it."

"It was wrong of her to say nothing. I wouldn't have minded. His relationship with Carolina was never a secret between us and I know how much he loved me."

"You two were lucky."

"We were. It's not often couples stay as close as we were for so long. I'll never replace him. I don't want to. How am I going to tell Jon?"

"Do you want me to tell him?"

"No, no ... thanks, but I think it should come from me."

"You look as if you could do with an Andrew special," he said.

"Whisky won't help, I have to drive back."

"I could take you."

She stood up and slipped her coat over her shoulders. "No ... sorry, but I need to be on my own."

"Are you sure you'll be all right."

"Of course, I just need to go home and have a think."

CHAPTER 33

Marion was the first one to appear in the church hall after Daisy the next morning. She had arrived with a cake-tin under her arm and a basket of raffle prizes. The tables had been set out the night before as arranged. Knitted bunting festooned the hall courtesy of the Sunday school. A giant hen with brown-painted feathers and two yellow chicks stared at her from the stage. "Do you like Matilda?" Daisy's voice seemed to be coming from inside the hen.

"Is that you, Daisy?"

Her head popped out and then her legginged legs. She scrambled off the stage brushing dust from her tunic. "It took me ages to paint the feathers last night. I should have been more careful when I put her in the shed after last year's fair. The chicks were ok, I'd bubble-wrapped them."

"The hall looks fantastic."

"Good. Your table's near the door."

"I know ... it's my job to catch everyone as they arrive," she said.

"You'll have an extra pair of hands this year. Thyme Sykes has offered to help. She can't do much standing or running round with her leg, but I thought she could help fold the tickets for you."

"Does Bella know?"

"I haven't told her."

"I hope she doesn't cause a scene."

"I'm sure she won't. Fr. Jon has been pouring oil on troubled waters."

"Thank goodness for that. I'll set out these prizes and then I can help you," she said taking the cake from its tin.

Daisy walked over to inspect the display. "That cake is fantastic ... I love the little nests. Well, I think I'm done. I've fired up the urn. Rachel said she'd be here early. We just need everyone else to turn up on time."

The chatter of voices was deafening as Diana arrived at the church hall. She could hear the squeaky voice of Mr. Punch above the babble and noticed a crowd of children sitting cross-legged on the floor giggling and clapping at his antics. As the knot of newcomers dissipated she saw Thyme seated behind at a picnic table, an ice cream tub full of change in front of her. "I see they've got you working," she said.

"I volunteered. This is about the only job I can do."

"How much is it?"

"Fifty pence to get in ... can I sell you some raffle tickets? The prizes are over there."

Diana followed her gaze to the table covered in bottles of wine, tins of biscuits and various soft toys arranged in order of size next to boxes of cosmetics and a giant basket of fruit. Marion's cake was sitting in the middle, decorated with sugared eggs in nests and a clutch of chicks. "I'll have six strips please. Did you meet Isobel Flynn? I hope I haven't missed her," she said scanning the hall for a glimpse of the guest of honour.

"I did. You haven't missed her. She brought her granddaughter with her. They're over there watching Ben's show."

"I'll get Jon to introduce me ... where is he?"

"He's around somewhere," Thyme said. "I've just seen him. Over there ... by the tombola."

"Ah yes ... he's coming over."

"Mum ... I thought you'd got lost. Come and have a cup of coffee," Jon said. "I've saved you a seat."

Thyme was concentrating on tearing off pink strips from the book of tickets in her hand. She didn't waver from her task, but Diana detected a rosy glow creeping over her cheeks. She unbuttoned her coat. "It's warm in here, isn't it?" she said taking the tickets. "Thanks, Thyme, see you later."

He guided her through the hall to an area cordoned off for refreshments. "Here we are," he said removing his leather jacket from one of the wooden seats borrowed from the church.

"It looks like you're going to make lots of money," she said.

"I hope so. Sorry I didn't have time to chat the other day."

"Don't worry about it. I understand. I'm glad Thyme's joining in. It must be pretty isolating not to be able to get about easily."

He stashed his jacket under one of the chairs. "I'm trying to make her feel part of the community," he said. "What did you want to discuss with me?"

"I like Thyme," she said. "She's had such a bad run of luck."

"You don't know the half of it," he said.

"Oh?"

"I can't tell you right now, but I'm trying to sort it out for her...so, what was it?"

"What was what?"

"What did you want to discuss with me?"

"Oh that ... yes ... well, I've decided to sell the flat and I've put in an offer on a small detached house in Cooper's Close."

"Really ... how come ... did you win the lottery?"

"In a way ... do you remember Granny Moffatt's Chinese vase, the one you and Dad tried to fly paper aeroplanes into?"

"Yes."

"Tom said I should put it in the auction."

"Right ..."

"It sold for an enormous amount of money."

"No way ..."

She nodded. “I know, fantastic, isn’t it?”

“I can’t believe it.”

“It’s true. Obviously I’ll give you some more towards the organ but with all that and my savings I can afford to buy the house.”

“What about the flat?”

“I’m putting it on the market to pay for the renovations. The little house needs a new kitchen, bathroom, everything. I want to do it all myself ... well, not the plumbing of course or the re-wiring, but all the decorating.”

“It sounds like it will take you years.”

“Probably; it’s what I need, Jon. The flat’s not the same without Dad. I need something to fill my time. If my offer’s accepted, I’ll move in and start the alterations after I’ve been away with Betsy. I might get her to help me. She’s good at D.I.Y. She can come and stay. I couldn’t ask her before. I don’t have a spare room in the flat, as you know.”

“Well, I’m really pleased for you but I hope you’ll organise a survey before you go ahead, avoid any nasty surprises.”

“It’s all in hand. I’ll be nearer the church. I might be able to help you. I don’t mind doing a bit of parish visiting. I’ve enjoyed helping Tom. It reminded me what it used to be like at the rectory.”

“I could do with an assistant; I’ve discussed curates with the Bishop but so far nothing’s on offer.”

“And what about Thyme ...”

“Thyme?”

“Come on, Jon. I get the feeling that you quite like her.”

He smiled and moved his head closer to hers. “Shhh,” he said. “It’s complicated.”

“Have you told her how you feel?”

“No and I can’t tell her.”

“I think she might feel the same way.”

“She doesn’t,” he said.

"How do you know if you haven't asked?"

"I didn't have to ask. She told me I was a good friend."

"'Good friends' is a start."

Joan Drabble was hovering behind them with a coffee pot. "Sorry to interrupt," she said "But Rachel told me to come and see if you needed a refill."

Diana pushed her cup towards her. "Thanks. Who made the shortbread?"

"Marks and Spencer," she said.

"It tastes home made."

"Marion made the scones. Fr. Jon?" she said lifting the coffee pot in his direction.

"Not for me, thanks. This is my third."

"No-one's counting."

He shook his head and she moved away. Diana tugged at his sleeve. "Faint heart never won fair maiden," she said. "I've got something else to tell you ... something about Dad and that really is complicated."

"How do you mean?"

"I don't want to go into it here. Come round tonight; I'll tell you then."

"It might not be till late."

"That's fine. You know I'm never in bed before twelve. Now, do you think you could introduce me to Isobel Flynn?"

"She asked about you."

"Did she?"

"She seemed to know about Dad dying."

"She probably knew him years ago before she moved up north."

"There she is," he said indicating a glamorous red-head sitting on one of the chairs near the stage with a toddler giggling on her knee. "Phoebe seems to be enjoying Punch's antics."

"It's a shame to interrupt the show."

They waited for Mr. Punch to bow to the hall and then as the audience gave him a round of applause they moved to Isobel's side. "My mother's here," he said.

Isobel smiled. "I've been looking forward to meeting you."

"I hope you didn't mind us turning one of your paintings into an organ."

"Not at all; it's nice to have it back in the family."

"Jon says you knew his father."

"Only by reputation; my son-in-law, Ian, knew him. Ian Chisholm."

"Of course, I didn't make the connection," she said.

"You must come back when the organ's in place; come and see how well we've spent the money," Jon said.

"I will. I know my husband would enjoy that. He's a great fan of church music."

"Have you had something to eat?" Diana said. "Would Phoebe like a biscuit or something?"

"I'd love a coffee and I'm sure Phoebe could manage a biscuit."

"Let's go and find a table," Diana said.

"I need to circulate," Jon said. "I'll leave you to it."

"You must be proud of him," Isobel said as he moved away.

"I am. He seems to be a big hit in this parish."

"He's charming and I'm told he works hard. A winning combination," Isobel said.

"He gets his charm from his father and the work ethic."

"And his good looks from his mother," Isobel said. "I hope you don't think this too forward of me but I'd really like to paint you. I've been doing a lot of portraits recently. Would you mind?"

"I'd be flattered."

"Give me your contact details. I'll be in touch."

"Coffee?" Joan said. "It's a new pot."

"Not for me, I've had my quota," Diana said.

“White, please,” Isobel said.

“Sugar’s on the table.”

“Are there any biscuits for Phoebe?” Diana asked.

“A rich tea or something,” Isobel said. “Pippa doesn’t like her to have too much sugar.”

“I’m sure there are some in the kitchen,” Joan said bustling off to look.

“I’ve got her juice in my bag ... here we are sweetie,” Isobel said as she settled Phoebe more comfortably on her knee. Phoebe took the lidded cup and sucked hard.

“She’s been very good,” Diana said.

“She’s a poppet. Do you have any grandchildren?”

Diana shook her head. “Jon’s an only child and he shows no signs of getting married.”

“Who’s that young woman he’s talking to now? They seem very friendly.”

“Thyme Sykes ... he says they’re just good friends but I’ve a feeling there’s more to it. I’d be the last one to know if there was anything going on ... he plays his cards very close to his chest.”

Isobel nodded. “My son’s exactly the same. It’s hard being left out of the loop, but in affairs of the heart men often need a bit of encouragement. It took ages for Adrian to see that we would be perfect together. Sometimes a little push works wonders.”

CHAPTER 34

There was a message from Jack Tighe when Diana got home from the fair. Her offer had been accepted. She rang Tom straight away but there was no reply. She smiled as she thought of a message she could leave for him. "It's Diana. I wanted you to know that the eagle has landed." It was an old cliché but she knew he'd understand and it might even make him laugh. Goodness knows he'd had little opportunity for that in the previous few days.

She was about to telephone Daisy with her news when she remembered that she would still be at the fair. Jon would be the first to hear about her investment and that was as it should be. She thought he'd be pleased her offer had been accepted. Her other news was more problematic. She wasn't sure how he would take that.

It was well after nine when he arrived. "Sorry I'm so late."

"It's not that late. I hope you did well this afternoon," she said.

"We won't know for certain until Daisy's had a chance to tot up all the extras and taken off the expenses," he said. "Any chance of a cuppa ... it's been a long day."

"The kettle's just boiled. My offer's been accepted."

"Oh ... the house you mean ... well done."

"I'm really looking forward to the project; I'm not ready to shut myself away with my knitting just yet. Come and sit down."

"What's this business about Dad?"

"It was very strange ... do you remember South America?"

"You mean his colourful past?"

"It was more colourful than you could imagine. I don't quite know how to put it. You see, now Mary's died Carolina has decided to spill some of the beans." She hesitated. "Look, there's no point making this anything other than it is. She had his child," she said.

His eyebrows flew up and he swore under his breath. "How long have you known about this?"

"Not long. Tom had an email from him the other day. He's coming over for Mary's funeral as his mother's representative. I know this must be difficult for you but it doesn't change anything."

"Of course it does ... I have a brother ..."

"Yes ... Philip Perez ... do you want to meet him?"

He got up and strode up and down the room. "Sorry Mum, but this is bizarre. First you tell me I have a brother and then you ask if I want to meet him. I can't tell you. I can't even take it in ... it's a massive shock. It's always been just the three of us ... two now."

"You don't have to meet him if you don't want to."

"Are you all right with all of this?"

"I was surprised ... well ... shocked like you; it was unsettling at first but it happened a long time ago, long before I met Dad. I know he loved me and that's all that matters. He loved you, too."

"Did he know about the child?"

"No, she didn't tell him she was pregnant; she came from a wealthy family. She didn't need his support to look after the baby."

"Does he know about me?"

"No."

He suddenly thought of Thyme. She had lost her baby. There could have been another lost baby had the circumstances been different. Did he want to meet his brother ... would he regret it if he didn't? What would she say? Would it hurt her all over again, bring back the bitter memories?

"What are you thinking, Jon?"

He couldn't tell her ... he didn't want to admit that Thyme was on his mind; that she was almost constantly on his mind. "I don't know."

"You don't have to make a decision right now. He won't be here for a few days."

"It might be awkward if I say, no. He'll see me at the funeral. It wouldn't be rocket science for him to work out who I am."

"You could speak to the Bishop ... get someone else to take the service."

"That would be a bit extreme. I guess we're meant to meet. It's just not something I ever contemplated ... having a brother."

"Would it be so bad?"

"Not necessarily but it would change who I am ... well, who I thought I was ..."

"You'll still be who you are. Who knows, you might get on well together."

"I need time to mull it over."

"Of course you do. Take your time. Talk it through with Tom."

"Yes, I might do that."

"Whatever you decide, I'll be right behind you."

After lunch the following day Diana called Daisy. "Are you in this afternoon?"

"Yes ... why ... I'm making marmalade," she said.

"I've got loads to tell you."

"Come round and keep me company it always takes forever to set."

"See you in about an hour.

"Can't wait ..."

She felt young, skittish as she drove along with The Phantom of the Opera blaring from the car stereo ... like she had when she first met Andrew; effervescent, drunk on life confident in her abilities.

Daisy's house was suffused with the delicious aroma of oranges as she pushed open the back door. "Daisy," she called. "Where are you?"

"Right here," Daisy said. She was wrapped in a flowery apron her hair held back by a chiffon scarf, stirring a bubbling pan, ten glass jars lined up on the work-top waiting to be filled. "I'm nearly done. I wouldn't have bothered doing this today but the lads finished the marmalade this morning and it wouldn't be breakfast without it."

"You could have nipped down to the supermarket."

"It's not the same, though, is it? Home-made is so much nicer. What's up?"

"I've got a surprise for you."

"Have you now ..."

"I'm buying Maggie Watt's house."

Daisy stopped mid-stir. "You're not ..."

"I am."

"I thought it was already sold."

"The chain broke at the last minute and the sale fell through."

"Wow ... can you afford it?"

"If you'd asked me that a couple of weeks ago I would have said, no, but something completely random happened. Do you remember my grandmother's vase?"

"You mean the big ugly one?"

"It wasn't so ugly after all. Tom said I should put it in the auction. Chinese porcelain is going crazy at the moment. That plus my savings made enough for me to buy the little house. I'm so looking forward to doing the renovations. I want to have a go at all the decorating myself."

"You're mad. It will take you forever."

"Let's face it Daisy, I've got forever haven't I? I was getting stir-crazy cooped up in that flat. It didn't seem so bad when Andrew was there but I haven't got room to do my painting. I can't have people to stay; there's no garden to potter in. It isn't me at all ... how's the marmalade?"

"I think it's done," she said dropping a teaspoonful of the sticky brew onto a cold saucer. "Yes ... perfect. What does Jon think about this madness?"

"He's ok with it."

"And the other piece of news, what did he think about that?"

"He took it in his stride ... I think he'll decide to meet Philip. Why wouldn't he? It might have been different if Andrew had still been alive, but now they can meet as equals."

"Good point."

"I wanted to talk to you about Jon. I think he needs our help."

"Does he?"

"Well, he seems quite keen on Thyme."

"I thought so ... that's the last jar. Let's sit down in the conservatory," Daisy said. She clicked the lid into place and rinsed her fingers under the tap.

"Lovely light in here," Diana said. "Have you ever thought of taking up painting?"

"No ... I'll leave that to you and Betsy. So what's Jon's problem?"

"He says it's complicated. How complicated can it be? He's not married. She's not married ... come on Daisy ... I can see you know something."

"I do, but you must promise not to tell him I told you."

"Cross my heart and hope to die."

"You remember that special service I mentioned to you the other day?"

"Yes."

"I know why he's doing it."

"Go on then."

"It's quite tragic. She had an abortion years ago. It's been haunting her ever since."

"No ... what happened?"

"She was engaged to Ollie ..."

"I know they split up and he went to New Zealand, I told you."

"Yes, but she was already pregnant before he went. He didn't want the child. He had planned to go without her, without even *telling* her. Her mother and her aunt persuaded her to say nothing to anyone and then her aunt took her up to Scotland to have an abortion. She was quite far on in the pregnancy by then. She had to give birth to the baby."

"Poor Thyme ... what was it?"

"A little boy; Jon's having trouble with the whole abortion thing. He understands why and how it happened but it goes against everything he believes. He suggested the service as a way of acknowledging the baby and for Thyme to have closure. It's on Friday evening."

"He must understand how difficult, how desperately sad it was for her."

"I think he does. I know he cares for her. I'm certain she cares for him. I've noticed how she gazes at him when she thinks no-one's looking but he's convinced himself that she only sees him as a friend, nothing more."

"That's what he told me, too. If they care so much for each other they must be meant to be together. Look what happened to Andrew and Carolina."

"If they had been meant to be together we wouldn't be having this conversation."

"No, I suppose not but I don't want Jon to miss his chance of happiness. I had a long chat with Isobel Flynn at the fair and she gave me an idea ..."

"Isn't she wonderful?"

"Yes ... she asked if she could paint my portrait."

Daisy laughed. "Me too ... what fun ... we could both have our portraits done and leave them in the attic to get older while we stay forever young."

"Daisy be serious ... as I was saying, she gave me an idea about Jon and Thyme."

"How do you mean?"

"We're going to have to play Cupid."

Daisy's eyes gleamed. "What did you have in mind?"

CHAPTER 35

Jon lit the last of the candles and then turned to take it all in. There were rows of tee-lights all round the altar and on the window sills either side of the church. It looked intimate, spiritual ... holy in their soft light and with the shadows dancing on the walls. “It’s good of you to arrange all this on your day off,” Daisy said.

“It was the only way I could be sure I wouldn’t be asked to do anything else.”

“Do you want me to stay?”

“I don’t mind. I’m not sure what Thyme will think.”

“I’ll wait in the vestry if she’d rather not. You’ll need help clearing up again. It’s such a sad story. I wish you’d told me before. I feel so sorry for her and little Matt.”

“She’s been haunted by the whole thing; put her life on hold all this time. It is sad.”

“It’s nearly six,” she said.

“I’d better robe up. Do you mind waiting here until I come back?”

“I’ll hand out the service sheets if someone turns up before then.”

“Thanks Daisy. Did I ever tell you that you’re an angel? I don’t know what I’d do without you.”

“Stop it,” she said. “Get changed.”

It was barely more than a minute before the iron handle rattled in the old oak door and it creaked open to reveal Ben and Bella arm in arm. “Good evening,” Daisy said. “It’s good to see you both. You’re here for Matt?”

“We are,” Ben said.

"We're here for Thyme, too."
"Well said, old girl."
"Would you like an order of service ... it's only short."
"Thanks ... where do you want us to sit?"
"Anywhere you like."
"Let's go up to the front," Ben said. "We'll be able to see better up there."
"I love all the candles," Bella said as they walked up the aisle together.
"Will this do you?" he said, shuffling into a seat two rows back from the front row of chairs.
She nodded and took her place beside him to read through the single sheet Daisy had given her. The door opened again and Thyme appeared with Neil, Chantal and the girls.
"Sit anywhere," Daisy said. "Fr. Jon will be with you in a minute."
"Thanks," Neil said.
"Would you rather I waited in the vestry, Thyme?" Daisy asked. "I don't mind."
"I'd like you to stay," she said. "I haven't had a chance to thank you yet ... for helping me after the accident."
"I was pleased to be able to do something. You looked so bad I was worried you wouldn't make it."
"I'm sorry I scared everyone."
"Well, you've recovered and that's the main thing ... I was touched by your story. This service is a great idea. Here's Fr. Jon now. I'll sit at the back."
"Welcome," he said. "Are we all here?"
Thyme scanned the tiny congregation. "I think so."
"Right, then we'll make a start." He walked up to the altar rail and faced the front. "It's good to see you all here this evening. We've come together to give thanks for baby Matthew's life. The birth of a child is a cause for celebration but tragically baby Matthew's life was cut short ... please stand

for the first prayer ...” he bowed his head. “Loving God you hold all things in life and call us into your kingdom of peace; help us to walk the path of truth and fill our lives with gratitude and faith, through Jesus Christ our Lord. Amen ... and now we’ll sit for the reading.”

He waited for Thyme to join him and stood silently at her side, sensing her nervous energy and her need for his support as she braced herself for the ordeal. He felt the light touch of her hand on his arm. Her body quivered as if she were taking strength from their connection. She coughed nervously. “This is a reading from the gospel of Luke,” she said.

‘*... They even brought babies for him to touch; but when the disciples saw them they scolded them for it. But Jesus called for the children and said, ‘Let the little ones come to me; do not try to stop them; for the kingdom of God belongs to such as these. I tell you that whoever does not accept the kingdom of God like a child will never enter it.’*

He squeezed her hand when she had finished, releasing it slowly as his gaze followed her back to her seat before he carried on with the service. “Alice and Amy would now like to read us a poem.” They got to their feet and he beckoned them towards him. “Come and stand up here with me,” he said. He waited while they put their heads together, whispering in each other’s ears behind protective hands. “We’re ready,” Alice said.

“Off you go.”

Alice held a piece of paper between them and Amy took one step forward. “This is a poem called ‘Lullaby’ by Alan Bold,” she said before stepping back next to her sister.

They both took a deep breath.

‘*Close your eyes gently And cuddle in, Keep yourself snug, a New day will begin.*

Have pleasant dreams about Those things you love, Sleep is an island Waiting above.

Night is a blanket Keeping you warm If you close your eyes you can Come to no harm.

Dreams are like journeys Drifting along, Rest is a present Keeping you strong.'

This time it was Alice who took a step forward. "Good night baby Matthew," she said and then they turned and walked silently back to their parents in single file.

"Thank you Alice and Amy. Now we'll have a moment of silence and reflection to make our own prayers to the Lord remembering the loved ones who are no longer with us ..." He waited for a few minutes after all the shuffling and squeaking of chair-legs had ceased. "Let us pray ... Heavenly Father, we praise you for baby Matthew; surround him with your blessing that he may know your love and be protected from evil ... and we pray for Thyme that she may find peace in your love.

Lord, help us to put down past burdens and show compassion for others; may we give thanks to the Lord for all the good things He has given us, be penitent for all the things we have done wrong and share our joy at His forgiveness ... Lord Jesus wipe our slates clean, clear our wrong-doing, give us all a fresh start. Let us remember that death is not the end but the beginning ... and now, we'll stand to say the Lord's prayer ... Our Father who art in heaven, hallowed be thy name, thy kingdom come ..."

All heads bowed and the murmur of voices praying brought a satisfactory conclusion to the simple service. Jon made the sign of the cross. "May the Lord bless you and keep you. May he shine the light of his countenance upon you and give you peace," he said and then he walked quietly towards the back of the church.

Neil and Chantal followed. “Thank you,” Neil said as he shook his hand.

“I hope it’s helped.”

“I think it has.”

They hovered by the door with the girls as Thyme stopped to speak to him, her eyes luminous with tears. “It was a lovely service, thank you.”

He took her hand and pressed it between his like a pansy in a press. “Was it what you wanted?”

“Yes ... it felt right. We’re going away for a few days, Neil, Chantal, the girls and me.

“Are you?”

“I promised Amy I’d take her to see the Kelpies.”

“Ahh ... Scotland.”

He felt a frisson of disappointment at being left out. She must have picked up on it. “Yes ... sorry ... I hope you don’t mind.”

His cheeks reddened and he was glad Daisy had not yet turned on the lights. “Why should I mind? You go and enjoy yourself. I’ve got a busy week preparing for Easter.”

“We’ll be back by the weekend. I’ll see you then. I must go, they’re waiting.”

“Have a good trip.”

The spiritual atmosphere was melting away as Daisy switched on the lights and extinguished the flames. Ben and Bella were lingering in the porch as Jon wandered outside to watch them all leave. “Good little service,” Ben said.

Bella gave him a hug. “Thank you,” she said. “I’ve been very stupid.”

“Have you spoken to your son?”

“Yes. He admitted that Thyme was telling the truth. I told her what he said and I apologised for not believing her. She cried and I felt even worse but at least it’s out in the open now. I did have a grandson once. All this has taught me a lesson. I’m going to try not to be so judgmental in future."

"We're planning a memorial stone for him in the garden and Ollie's coming over in the summer to see it," Ben said.

"And how are you both now?"

"Getting there," Ben said. "It's been hard for her, hasn't it old girl?" he added as he put an arm round Bella's shoulders. "But we're in this together. We were all to blame for that little boy's death."

"I hope the service has brought you some closure."

"It has," she said.

Ben nodded. "It's what we needed."

CHAPTER 36

"I thought you might like to see the house," Diana said the following week as she chatted with Jon on the phone.

"I would, very much."

"Maggie's moved out now. I asked if I could have the key tomorrow afternoon. "Can you be there for about four thirty?"

"I should be able to pop over for half an hour."

"I'll meet you there."

"Well," he said looking down at the cat. "I'm going to suss out 'the project' tomorrow." She stared back at him with a quizzical expression. "What have you got to say about that ... is she mad?"

Pandora rose unsteadily to her feet and seemed to wink knowingly before turning her back on him and sauntering over to her box where she promptly fell asleep.

"You're right, as always ... do what you can while you can. She'll be fine."

The following afternoon was grey and unpromising. The misty drizzle looked as if it might turn into a downpour at any minute. Diana and Jon arrived at the house at almost the same time. "The garden's a bit of a mess," he said.

"It's not a problem; you know I love gardening. I'm looking forward to seeing what's hidden under all the dead wood. It's just the right time of year to do something about it. Come into the lounge ... there's an open fire."

"Hmm," he said peering up the blackened chimney. "It seems to be stuffed with old telephone directories."

"I think Maggie had lost the plot."

"Are you sure it's not too much for you, Mum."

"You're treading on dangerous ground there ... of course it's not."

"I can definitely see the potential."

"That's not the best bit," she said tugging him into the back room. "Look at the window seat and the French windows. The light will be perfect for painting."

"What about the kitchen?"

"Workable but in need of up-dating," she said moving aside to let him through.

He took in the tired work surfaces and scuffed floor. "Hmm ... I see what you mean."

"You know, it's been a long time since I've felt so enthusiastic about anything ... and I'm just over the road from Daisy. She said she'd come round while we were here ... to see the house now it's empty."

"Will you like having her so close?"

"Yes. It will be fun."

"You might have to get some of your furniture back from Cath."

"I won't need much. I'm buying new. The old stuff would have been too big anyway. Come and see the bedrooms," she said as she made her way back into the hall and waited for him to follow her up the stairs. "You'll understand what I mean ... no room for those enormous wardrobes."

"I loved those wardrobes. They were great for hide and seek."

"Your Narnia days are over," she said as she opened the door to the room which she had ear-marked for herself. "This could be lovely with a lick of paint and some new curtains."

He strode over to the window. "Great view; you can see right over to the fishing lakes."

She led the way across the landing. "This room's a touch smaller and the view's not as good, but don't you just love that fireplace?" she said staring fondly at a small cast-iron fireplace with a minuscule grate.

"It's ok," he said. "I hope you know what you're doing, Mum."

She smiled up at him. "I do ... I really do. You don't have to worry."

"Ok ... well ... I'd better make tracks. It's the washing of feet service this evening."

"Wait a minute ... are you all right after what I told you about Dad and Carolina?" she said as they re-traced their steps.

"I think so."

"It was rather a shocker."

"I'm just getting my head round the long-lost brother angle."

She reached out for his arm. "It won't change things between us."

"Of course not but it is a bit crazy."

"With the age difference I knew your father had a life before we met. We didn't keep things from each other. I'm certain that if he'd known about Philip he would have told me."

"And you ... are you all right about it?"

"It's strange and I don't know why, but I half expected something like this would happen. Your father was very charismatic in his early days. I'm quite excited to meet Philip."

"I don't know if I'm excited. I'm more curious. I want to see what he looks like."

"So do I."

"Hello."

He spun round as Thyme appeared at the front door. Diana did not seem surprised at all. "Is Daisy with you?" she said.

"No, she had to take a phone call. She sent me over to tell you she's not going to make it."

"Oh dear ... I hope everything's all right. I'd better go and check. Here's the key, Jon, lock up for me would you?" she said and whisked out of the house before he had time to respond.

"I didn't know you were back," he said.

"We came back last night."

"How are you ... how did it go?"

"Good, thanks. It's getting very dark in here."

"I think we're in for some thunder." He tried the light switch, flicking it up and down several times in quick succession to no avail.

"The electricity must have been turned off. It probably needs re-wiring anyway. Mum will have her work cut out getting this place sorted."

"It has oodles of character," she said wandering towards the morning room. "You don't mind if I have a nosey about do you? I love looking round old houses."

They could hear rain pounding on the roof of the lean-to shed and then there was an awkward silence as neither of them knew what to say next. "I think we've been stitched up," he said. "I apologise for my mother ... shall we go?"

"I'd rather wait until the rain goes off. I don't have a coat. Daisy came to fetch me in her car. My leg is still a bit weak. I thought I'd be getting a lift back."

"We can't even sit down," he said.

"There's the window seat."

Rain was battering the back of the house, rolling down the window like marbles down a run. He tried not to sit too close to her. "Um ... how did it go in Scotland ... I mean ..." he didn't know what he meant. He felt tongue-tied and stupid, cross with himself for having asked her the same question twice.

She didn't seem to notice. "It went very well, thanks ... Amy loved the sculpture but it wasn't as good as our weekend ... I missed you."

"Sorry ... what did you say?" It was so dark now he couldn't make out her expression.

"I missed you," she repeated. "I'm glad the electricity's off;

it's a lot easier making a fool of yourself in the dark ... I want you to know how much you've helped me ..." she added as lightning lit up the room and for a minute he could see her sincerity as well as hear it "... how grateful I am for everything you've done for me and how much I love spending time with you. I knew it already but being up there in Scotland without you made me really miss you ... I love you, Jon. It doesn't matter if you don't feel the same way. I needed you to know."

"I thought we were just good friends."

"Not *just* good friends." She shuffled a bit nearer as thunder rumbled in the distance and he could no longer resist the urge to take her in his arms and kiss her in the way he had wanted to for weeks. Her lips were sweet, responsive; he kissed her eyes, her nose, her cheeks and she clung to him as if she would never let him go.

"Are you sure this is what you want?" he said, his voice muffled in her hair.

"More than anything," she said. "But I'm scared ..."

He pulled away slightly "... scared? What are you scared of ... not me?"

"No, not you ... of the future, I mean."

"This is a leap of faith for me, too. I can't guarantee what will happen, no-one can."

"I thought Ollie and I would be together forever. It was just wishful thinking ... the dream of a romantic teenager. It didn't end well, as you know."

"That Thyme was a completely different person from the one you are now and I'm not Ollie. When you're young you think you're invincible, you never consider the future, or if you do, everything stays rosy. You get better at life as you get older."

"Yes ..." she said dreamily "You're right."

"You know a similar thing happened to my Dad when he was young."

"How do you mean?"

"Well he met a girl, Carolina years before he met Mum. She was on holiday over here from Argentina. He followed her to South America and then she sent him packing but she didn't tell him she was pregnant."

"Did she keep the baby?"

"She did and this is the bizarre thing, I've got a brother, Philip Andrew Perez; I'm going to meet him for the first time soon."

"That must be really strange ... to be told you have a brother you knew nothing about."

"It's bonkers. I'm still a bit stunned. I mean you read about these things in the Sunday papers but there have never been any dark secrets in our family ... well obviously there were, but we didn't know about them. You think your life is normal, like everyone else's and then something like this happens."

"That's how I felt about Ollie and Matt. I thought we had it made. He thought the opposite and I had to re-think the whole scenario. I had to *un*-think it."

He took her hand. "Look, I reckon if we both go into this relationship honestly with our eyes open and with a sense of commitment, there's no reason why it shouldn't last ... if we want it to. Will you marry me ... one day?"

She was smiling in the dark, now. "Maybe ... one day ... when my leg's better and everyone has got used to the idea that we're together."

"That's the thing," he said. "We can't be 'together' until we are married."

"Oh."

"Is that a problem?"

"I don't know."

"I want you to think about it; re-think it if you must but whatever you do, don't *un*-think it, please." She laughed. "Being a vicar's wife sort of means you belong to the parish, as

I do. You don't get much privacy. Everyone has an opinion about the way you live your life and they don't mind telling you what it is."

"It can't be that difficult. Your mum and dad seemed very happy."

"They were. How long do you need?"

"How long do I need?"

"Before you give me an answer; I want us to be together, Thyme. I haven't felt like this about anyone before. I need to know."

"When I know, you'll know," she said.

"Fair enough," he said. "Will it be this year?"

"Next year ... sometime ..."

"You're not going to say, never ..."

"No. I'm going to say ... yes."

He was staring out of the window watching the clouds and praying as he had never prayed before. He saw a watery sun appear as the clouds parted. It took him barely a second to understand her meaning. His face cracked into a smile and he turned to face her. Now the whole room seemed to be a ball of light with her at the epicentre. He felt warmth in his cheeks, his heart, in every part of him. "You will marry me?"

"Yes, I will marry you."

"In that case you had better come and meet Pandora."

"Who's she?"

"The other female in my life ... apart from my mother," he said and then he smiled at her confusion. "Pandora is my cat ... I hope you like cats."

"Hmm ... let me see," she said as her eyes danced. "I'll have to think about that one."

Ben was watching as they left Cooper's Close hand in hand after the storm. He smiled to himself. "There's something going on, there," he muttered as he trundled down the stairs.

"Guess what I've just seen, Bella," he shouted at the top of his voice.

"I don't know. You're always seeing things."

"Fr. Jon and Thyme walking down the road together ... I mean *together*."

"I could have told you there was something going on there. I said to Angela there was no point introducing him to Georgia. 'He's already spoken for', I said. She wasn't pleased."

"Georgia and Fr. Jon ... oh no ... no ... that wouldn't do at all."

"Well, you don't need to worry. He's with Thyme and perhaps she'll find some happiness at last."

"You don't know how pleased I am to hear you say that, old girl ..." he said grinning broadly, his wrinkles coming together like dough in a bowl " ... very pleased indeed."